Leithers: Two Families

William Haddow

Published 2023 CamusStone Press
Text Copyright© 2023 William Haddow
Edited by Ellie Owen – Rowanvale Books
Illustrations - Ionawr Davies
Cover design by Richie Cumberlidge - Morevisual Ltd

ISBN: 978-1-7392567-0-8

For Heather and Callum

Background

From the Programme Notes of the "Leithers Live" Theatre Production

How "Leithers" Happened

The inspiration for the first novel in the series, *Leithers – One Family* came from the archaeological dig in Leith's Constitution Street. Three hundred and five bodies were exhumed from a medieval cemetery, and through facial reconstruction techniques we learned how these people looked. I got to thinking how some of these individuals might have lived in medieval times, and that led to a few of them eventually appearing in the book.

Delving into Leith's history, I soon discovered all these remarkable stories, and the more I dug the more I found. Turns out that Leith is really quite unique in terms of the length and breadth of its fascinating history. I don't believe there is another town in the whole UK that can match it, apart from the ancient capital cities. Though, it was really only through a quirk of geography that Leith didn't become the ancient capital of Scotland itself.

The book was also about who you are. We see old black-and-white photos of dozens of men with big moustaches and cloth caps alongside women in big dresses and huge hats. All these people are now gone, but they all must have had interesting lives. We all have a long line of ancestors, just like the Prestons, and whether we realise it or not, they have contributed to who and what we are.

Inspiration also came from other authors: Ken Follett's *Pillars of the Earth* (1989), the story of the building of a medieval cathedral where a main character is the place itself, also *Saigon* (1982), Anthony Gray's novel about the Vietnam war, which offers an excellent example of how telling the story of a fictional family can be an effective way of teaching history.

Bill Haddow, May 2022

Leithers – Two Families
The second volume in the "Leithers" series

1832 – Leith's Story Retold.

New industry brings great opportunities to the port, but what lurks
in its dark underbelly?
Murder and mud, hardship and hope, pollution and pandemic,
crime and the kirk.

A tale of two families, in love and at war.

Who can tell what is lost in the swirling mists of time?
Maybe this is just how it happened.

List of Characters

McColligans
Abraham McColligan (deceased)
Flossie McColligan, his wife, 35
William McColligan, 16
Lark McColligan, 15
Eck McColligan, 14
Andy McColligan, 12
Eliza McColligan, 9

Prestons
John Preston (deceased)
Edith Preston, his wife, 37
Earnest Preston (deceased)
Tommy Preston, 18
Charlie Preston, 16
Henry Preston, 14
Sam Preston, 14
Annie Preston, 9

Others
Archie McTavish, a merchant
Dr Thomas Latta, a doctor
Superintendent Andrew Angus, Leith Police Chief
Bunty Angus, his wife
Constable Ross, Leith Police
Arabella Deveraux, a courtesan
Grannie O'Malley, a Vinegar Close resident
Tin Pan Aggie, a Vinegar Close resident
Big Zander McFarlane, a member of the McColligan gang
Deeks, a member of the McColligan gang
Mr Black, a fraternity member

The Kirk Session
Right Reverend Donald McIntosh, Parish Minister, South Leith Church
Reverend Allan Ponsonby, Junior Minister, South Leith Church

Lord Haddington, a landowner and factory owner
Deacon Johnston, Senior Deacon, South Leith Church
Alexander Preston, banker/financial adviser to the Kirk Session
Alan White, Police Commissioner and future Provost of Leith town council

Scots Dialect – Glossary

Aboot – *about*
Auld – *old*
Awfy – *awful*
Bairn – *child*
Baccy – *tobacco*
Bahookie – *buttocks*
Cannae – *can't*
Couried – *cuddled*
Dinnae – *don't*
Didnae – *didn't*
Doon – *down*
Dug – *dog*
Fae – *from*
Girning – *crying*
Hoose – *house*
Ken – *know*
Laddies – *boys*
Lassies – *girls*
Maw – *mother*
Midden – *rubbish dump*
Naw – *no*
Neuk – *small enclosed space*
Puss – *face*
Oor – *our*
Oot – *out*
Telt – *told*
Toon – *town*
Wee – *small*
Wha – *who*
Whit – *what*
Wisny – *wasn't*
Yin – *one*

Author's Note

This novel's journey started with a post that popped up on the 'Spirit of Leith' Facebook page, followed by an extensive period of digging to see what else was hidden there.

The book is a work of fiction; however, our tale is built around the lives of some real Leithers. The historical notes at the back offer further details of the limited information we have about their lives, but—SPOILER ALERT—you are advised to read the book first, as these notes may give away the details of some plot lines.

Our tale takes place in 1832, towards the end of the first industrial revolution, a period of massive social change driven by forces of technology and capitalism as the country moved (at times painfully) from an agrarian to an industrialised society.

As in the first *Leithers* novel, much effort has been made to provide an accurate historical background. I have leant heavily on sources such as Sue Mowat's seminal work *The Port of Leith: Its History and Its People* (2003), along with the work of James Scott Marshall, who wrote several books about Leith, on this occasion *Old Leith – The Caring Community* (1979) and *Old Leith at Work* (1977). If you want to know the real, rather than a dramatised, history of Leith, I would recommend these and other older volumes. Unfortunately, some of these are now quite difficult to find, so hopefully this *Leithers* historical series will offer some very limited compensation. Many, many websites have also been consulted on a wide range of diverse subjects, everything from 19th-century factories to church governance and paddle steamer design.

Significant inspiration was also drawn from the remarkable work, Henry Mayhew's *London Labour and the London Poor* (1850), which offers a detailed insight into the lives of the urban poor and destitute in the early/mid-19th century at a time before any kind of effective welfare provision.

For dramatic effect, I have taken some liberties with the chronology, in that those real events around which the story revolves happened a couple of years, rather than weeks, apart. If you spot any other historical errors, as with the first book in the series, please forgive them and accept this as an (occasionally dark) love letter to Leith—part two.

Bill Haddow, Jan 2023

Geography

The backdrop of this novel is old Leith (see map), little of which still exists. The cover of the book is from an 1839 print, but the Shore, harbour and pier wouldn't have looked much different a few years earlier in 1832.

In the 1880s, a major improvement project led to the development of the Henderson Street area, hundreds of modern tenements built in a scheme which swept away eighteen ancient closes and lanes of old Leith. Further demolition of much of the rest was to follow.

Originally, the river at Leith was tidal. Its depth varied daily, and at times would almost dry up. In 1969, a sea lock was installed, and the harbour and river were transformed into what we know today.

The key players in our tale live in:

Vinegar Close – Which ran between 34 Giles Street and 21 Yardheads. The line of the close was through the kids' park in Henderson Street to the side wall of the Vaults. The close was built by Henry Smith, a vinegar maker. A tablet from above a doorway can be found in the Edinburgh Museum courtyard in the Canongate.

St Leonard's Lane – The lane ran between where Henderson Street and Coalhill are now. This area of Leith was at one time known as Saint Leonard's Lands.

Note

This novel contains some language and attitudes which may have been more acceptable in 1832 but are less so today. These in no way reflect the attitudes or views of the author.

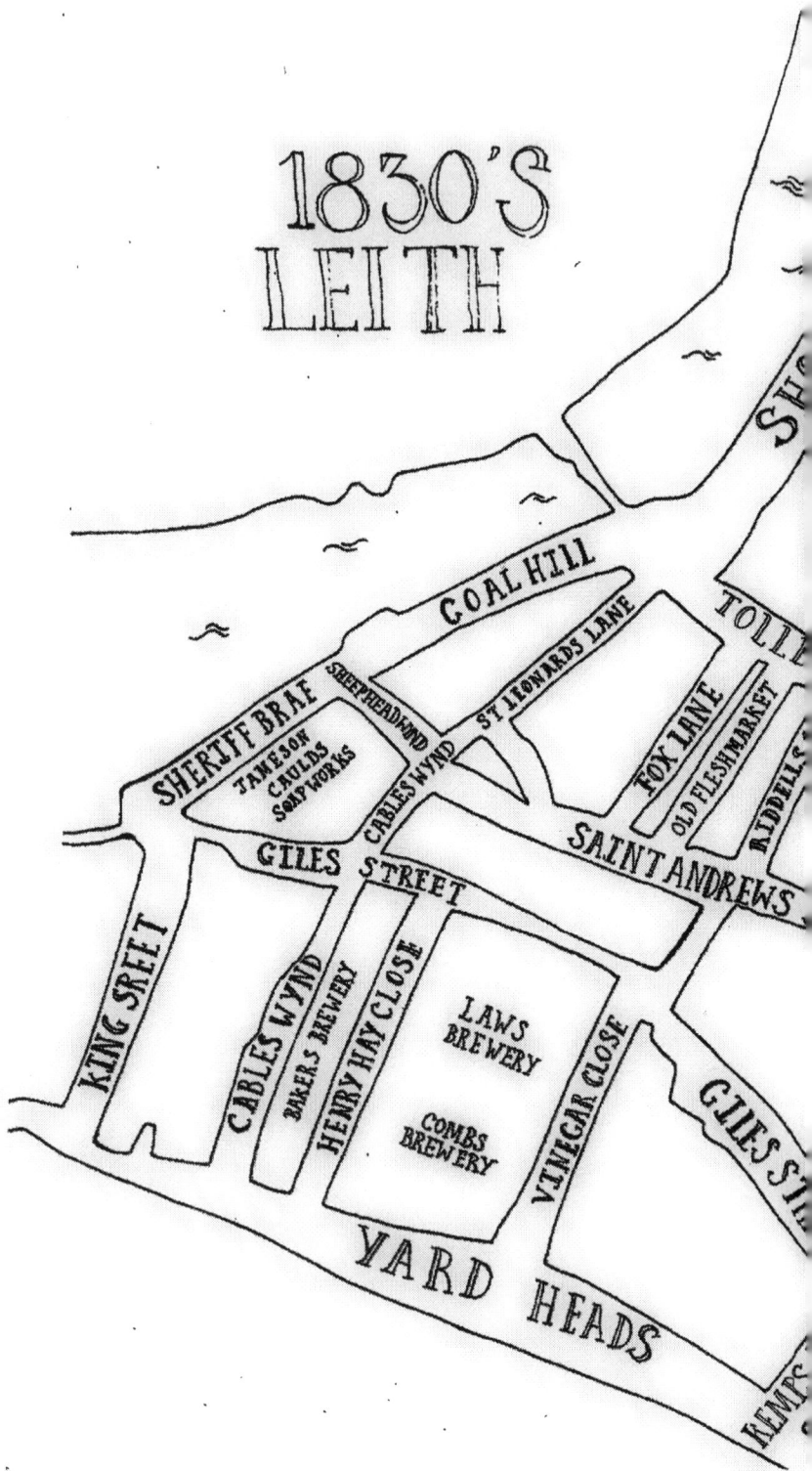

1830'S LEITH

COAL HILL

SHEPHEADWND

ST LEONARDS LANE

SHO

TOLL

SHERIFF BRAE

JAMESON CAULDS SOAPWORKS

CABLES WYND

FOX LANE

OLD FLESHMARKET

RIDDELLS

GILES STREET

SAINT ANDREWS

KING SREET

CABLES WYND

BAKERS BREWERY

HENRY HAY CLOSE

LAWS BREWERY

COMBS BREWERY

VINEGAR CLOSE

GILES ST

YARD HEADS

KEMPS

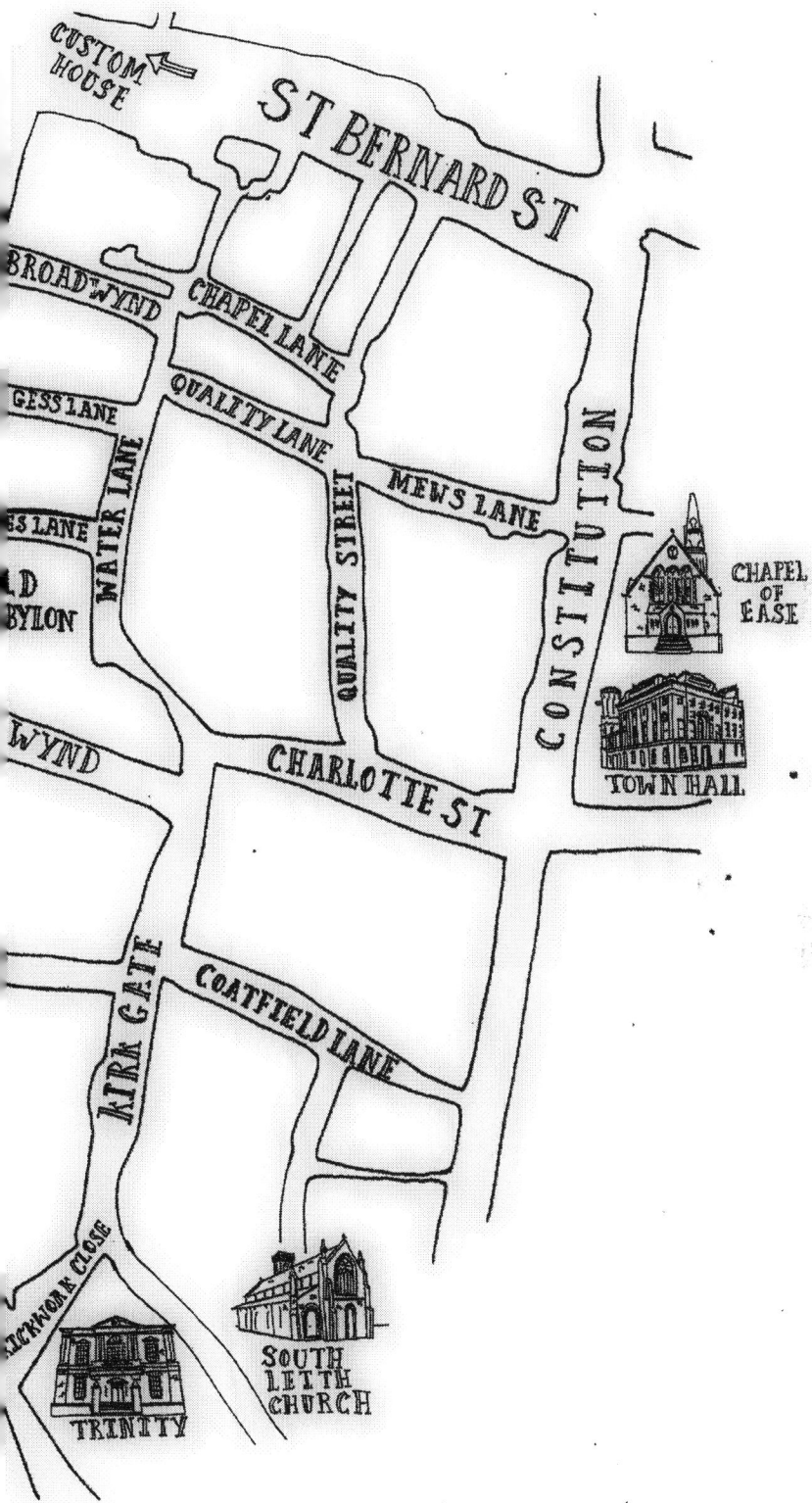

CUSTOM HOUSE

ST BERNARD ST

BROADWYND

CHAPEL LANE

GESS LANE

QUALITY LANE

WATER LANE

MEWS LANE

ES LANE

LD BYLON

QUALITY STREET

CONSTITUTION

CHAPEL OF EASE

TOWN HALL

WYND

CHARLOTTE ST

KIRK GATE

COATFIELD LANE

ICKWOOD CLOSE

TRINITY

SOUTH LEITH CHURCH

1. The Prelude
Leith 1832

Charlie Preston

Whenever Charlie had asked why, nobody seemed able to remember, but the problems had started long before the murder of both the fathers.

The arrangement was, and still is, that the Prestons owned the streets near the river and the McColligans the ground around the Yardheads and Kirkgate. It usually kept them apart.

Then, a few months back, things became heated when, one morning, young Charlie found a nice pewter jug in the river mud. He left it on the quayside, and William McColligan crept along and nicked it.

That evening, an altercation ensued when Charlie's dad, John, went to complain at the McColligans' place off Vinegar Close. He and William's father argued, then knifed each other in the guts. Very messy, reported Charlie's older brother Tommy when he returned home. "Loads of blood. Caused a right hullabaloo."

"I telt him not to take the knife," Edith, Charlie's maw, had said. "But as usual he was too drunk to listen."

Edith said the Prestons should never speak to the McColligans again. Best keep themselves to themselves.

And that's how it had been ever since.

2. Archie Considers
Thursday 1st March

Archie McTavish

Dawn. Archibald McTavish's considerable frame waddled along the cobbles on the Shore, terrier at his heels. The fur on her face was stiff with matted blood. Archie shivered, colder today. A thick harr shrouded the port, the moist air heavy with the smell of salt, seaweed and sewage. The river low, the sound of early morning carts rumbling in the gloom, horses jerking their heads and stomping.

Archie (known locally as Fat Archie—though never to his face) turned into Broad Wynd. His spirit lifted. He'd always enjoyed the way his gold leaf lettering stood out along the row of bakers, ship chandlers, bootmakers, apothecaries and other small stores that stretched up the lane of narrow, timber-fronted tenements: *Archibald McTavish – dealer in fine wares*.

A squeal as he kicked at shapes huddled in the doorway under an old scrap of canvas.

"Scram, you little scamps."

The terrier growled, and there was a blur as the three scrawny, ragged children curled together like kittens untangled and scrambled away. Archie's second kick missed, his enormous gut swinging.

He unlocked the bolt, and the door creaked open. Archie's shop stunk the familiar stink, packed to the rafters with shelves of old bottles, a few nicknacks, piles of rags, heaps of aged bones and bales of horsehair.

He set and lit the fire, then opened the gate into the enclosed yard out back. There, mounds of old rope, bent nails, other assorted rusting iron, a few chunks of copper and rolls of ancient canvas. He could hear the shuffle, coughs and grunts of the neighbours as they woke to another dawn in the cramped tenements above that encircled the yard. Bluebell, his terrier, with a wag of her tail, was grateful to receive the juicy bone he threw into her kennel. She'd earned it.

Archie filled the kettle from the water barrel and moved back inside, placed it on the hearth. He opened the sack collected the day before from that big house near the links and drew out a smart, almost new, dark green frock coat. He took the battered top hat from the shelf above and gave it a cursory brush, stepped in front of the mirror in the corner, and dragged a grubby hand through his greasy mop of tangled hair. A smile creased his heavy-lidded eyes as he bared yellowing, cracked teeth.

He'd visited the barber yesterday. He examined his smooth chin and squeezed the two boils. Not quite ready to burst yet, he decided. Quick pick at the left nostril of his bulbous, blackhead-flecked nose before slipping on the coat and placing the hat on his head with care.

He studied the mirror and patted his great belly. *Not bad*, he thought. *You, Archibald are a fine-looking man.* He scraped a piece of long dried snot from the moustache that mirrored his bushy sideburns.

"Smart threads for a wee bit flirtation," he said aloud before slipping the clothes off as the water for his tea began bubbling in the hearth.

He returned to the counter with the cup, a crease between his brows as he lifted the nib and considered what he was going to say. The speech he would give that he hoped offered an invitation she couldn't refuse.

Not long now, thought Archie. Maybe that nice little cottage across the river, the two of them. Even an outside chance of solving the puzzle of the small box. Years ago now, he'd last seen it, but he still remembered the red dragon mother-of-pearl design on the lid. That remained a mystery.

3. The Morning Call
Friday

Charlie Preston

"Charlie," said his maw. "Get them moving, the tide will be oot."

"Right, Ma. C'mon you lot, time to go."

No fuel for the fire today, so cold breakfast. Edith Preston cut the oatmeal squares from the porridge drawer. A ragged scrum of stiff shirts formed around her, each caked in yesterday's dried mud.

St Leonard's Lane, chilly but clear, maybe sun later. The usual early hubbub. Scrawny children setting out westwards to the mills for another long shift barged aside two shuffling beggars heading to their pitch, caps in hand. A group of barrow boys were off to battle with other costermongers at the morning market to find something to sell.

Charlie's slender frame stepped outside. With unhurried, casual movements, he stretched, breathed the dawn air and drew his hand through his tousled mop. A whiff of river sewage gelled with the lingering odour of boiled whale blubber from Jameson and Auld's soap works on Sherriff Brae and the fruity, yeasty, stink of the breweries, underpinned by the familiar stink from the tenement closes: spoiled vegetables, stale urine, and old animal fat. The low early morning murmurs were pierced with a sudden high-pitched whistle in the distance from the big steamer waiting at the harbour mouth.

The Prestons' street was a crooked lane of scruffy tenements, four storeys high and home to one hundred and eighty-two families. Basements filled with stinking refuse for which they had been a receptacle for years. Buildings with broken stairs, fallen plaster and damp, porous bricks.

All five Preston youngsters aimed for the river. They passed through a group of adults and children hurrying together for the ropeworks, then jostled with mothers with arms full of grubby linen heading for the standpipe in Tollbooth Wynd for wash day.

Tommy, short and stocky, was the oldest at eighteen; Charlie, tall and gangly, two years younger. Wee Annie, the youngest at nine, protesting, towed by the wiry frames of twins Henry and Sam, four years older. They turned into Sheephead Lane, then along Coalhill. It hadn't rained for days, and the river was a narrow sluggish stream, tide well out—perfect.

Two paddle steamers were by the quayside, a large one, new-painted and grand looking, and a small one, rusted and with worn wood. Alongside them, a smart three-masted clipper with sleek lines had keeled over at an angle, sails drooping away from the wharf, immobile in the mud.

Tommy gave the orders. "Henry and Sam, you start oot on the sandbar at the river mouth. Charlie, round the clipper. Annie, you sort the coal and iron. I'll do the steamers."

There was cloud but little wind. Wisps of grey smoke from early morning chimneys drifted then dispersed over the river as the Prestons climbed down the ladder into the stinking, oozing mud. Wasn't too cold today. Soon, they'd spread out along the river's edge under the quay, each stooped, peering into the mire and wading through puddles by the side of the meandering brown stream.

Early success came when Charlie found four copper nails near the bow of the clipper. Bits of coal were hoisted into their bags. Scraps of wood, aged rope, a little iron, and best of all, late on as the tide was rising, a new short plank of oak came floating right into Tommy's hands. A productive day.

They lifted their finds and went round to Archie's Scrap on Broad Wynd. The Prestons stood together with muddy slush dripping from their ragged clothes, a pool forming around bare feet.

"How many times have I telt you? Get ootside, I dinnae want you mud people messing up my shop."

Archie's great bulk bore down on them and he chased them out.

"Lay it oot." He pointed at the ground.

They presented their river pickings: a pile for rope, one for the wood and a third for iron and copper nails. The coal they would sell themselves later around the doors.

Archie's broad chin jutted. He scratched his greasy face with his greasy hand before pulling it through greasy hair.

"Tuppence for the rope, four and a ha'penny for timber, sevenpence for the nails."

"Aw, c'mon, Archie," protested Tommy.

"Enough!" Archie raised his hand and took a swipe. Tommy ducked. "Take it or leave it."

Charlie took the coins and pocketed them. They'd started moving off when the McColligans came around the corner from Water Lane with their day's street pickings. The Prestons stood outside Archie's booth, holding their ground, the McColligans a few yards off. They eyed each other, but said nothing this time. On the last occasion, it had become a confrontation, howls, fists and insults thrown in a brief skirmish.

The McColligans' crew, William at their head, ugly but not particularly tall. Solid, with muscle, dressed smarter than the others, who wore grubby short jackets and shirts. He was in a battered stovepipe hat and newish-looking blue tailcoat.

Three brothers: William, Eck and Andy, descending in size, but each with the same wide, thuggish face. Full lips, big flat noses and that carrot-orange hair. Alongside them were two of their sidekicks. The lumbering, gibfaced[1] Big Zander McFarlane, all saliva and brawn, and Deeks, dark eyes and that sly look of someone who would slit their mother's throat for a shilling.

Charlie thought them an unattractive bunch. Experience and the fading two-week-old bruise on his chin told him it was best to avoid a tangle if possible.

Behind them was the oldest sister, with that flame red hair, a distinct shade from the rest. Charlie caught her eye, and couldn't help a thin smile.

"Whit are you smiling at, Preston?" growled William, a harsh frown on his wide lips. He made a stride forward. Charlie took a step back.

"Whit's it to you, McColligan?" said Tommy, stepping to the front.

Then silence, for a full fifteen seconds, until the Prestons turned and headed for home.

---

1   *Gibfaced (19ᵗʰ cent) – Ugly person, especially with heavy lower jaw.*

4. Lark at Work
Saturday

Lark McColligan

For Lark McColligan, it had been a profitable morning. With her sack half full, she turned into the lane toward Fat Archie's scrap shop just after noon. Lithe like a cat, with dusty bare feet, gliding with a light, fluid step, observers were reminded of a stage dancer, other than that she walked with eyes scanning the ground. Pale, delicate features, freckles and flame red hair, dressed in the usual shabby plain brown woollen dress over a grubby linen petticoat. When working, she wore her best blue bonnet.

Lark could turn her hand to any task to earn a crust. However, her favoured trade was that of a collector of old cigar ends. She knew the choicest spots outside the taverns and places of entertainment or on street corners. The steps of McKenzie's shipyard office and the door of the Custom House. Anywhere that men gathered, they tended to smoke, and where they smoked, they tended to leave their tabs.

Lowered eyes brought other benefits, useful stuff found. Today, a discarded newish bonnet and strand of bacon fat that only needed a quick rinse at the public tap in Brickwork Close before scoffing for breakfast.

Owing to his reputation, she of course found Fat Archie unnerving, and so was always glad to complete the transaction as promptly as possible. Though in his defence, he often gave a fair price for old tobacco. She wondered what he did with it. Assumed he sent it somewhere to be made into more cigars.

She entered to find a tall gentleman stood at the counter with sharp features and narrow sideburns, well turned out in a smart coat and top hat, an unusual customer for Archie's scrap shop. He spoke in educated, clipped tones.

"Visited that apothecary two doors up, then noticed you've an excellent choice of old bottles."

"Oh, aye, doctor," said Archie with a fawning smile. "Only the best quality objects are available at McTavish's Fine Wares."

"I'm carrying out a range of experiments up at our dispensary, and these could come in very handy for my various chemical concoctions."

Archie rubbed his hands together in anticipation at the unexpected sale. He grinned through yellow teeth. "And how are the proposals for your new hospital progressing?"

"Ha, despite a lack of funds, we are moving forward, though still in the early stages," said the gentleman. "I'm afraid my colleagues and I will stick with working at our little Kirkgate dispensary at present."

They completed the transaction, the gentleman left; the door banged, another entered. Stocky and broad, sporting a smart blue jacket with the insignia of the Leith Police on the shoulder. He brushed past Lark as if she wasn't there. Stood at the counter, ruddy faced and stern with a neat moustache, he peered along a crooked boxer's nose.

"Well, well, Archie. And how are you this fine day?"

"Ah, Superintendent Angus, how awfy pleasant that you called. Things couldn't be better," said Archie, smiling. "And how is your dear wife and those lovely lassies of yours?"

The Superintendent's eyes narrowed.

"More sugar gone missing," he said. "Casks of whisky nicked, Persian carpets lifted, a watchman at McKenzie's boatyard knocked out cold. Three entire stacks of best mahogany vanished. Any information about that, by any chance?"

"All I can propose is a search of my yard oot back and then step oot front and read the sign above my door," said Archie dismissively. "You are well aware, sir, that says that I'm a dealer of fine wares, a respectable proprietor wha pays rates and taxes."

Superintendent Angus leaned forward, dark eyes creased, a hard glare.

"Can smell you in more ways that just your breath, McTavish." He brought his face close. "But one day you will slip up, and then I'll have you. You realise how that's likely to end."

Archie stepped back and put his hand to his brow in a dramatic expression of mock dismay. "I'm flabbergasted. Appalled that you might even suggest such a thing."

"I'm watching you, McTavish," said the Superintendent, pointing. He spun, took a brief check of Archie's yard, then barged out the front door.

Lark had to step back quickly to avoid being knocked over. Then, felt a jab of surprise when, rather than his customary scowl, Archie looked up and smiled. She ignored it, grabbed the bottom of her bag and emptied the pile on the counter. Aware it was a good haul, worth at least fivepence, she was prepared to do battle if offered any less.

"Whit a pair, eh?" said Archie with a smirk. "The mutton shunters[2] and the medical profession. Superintendent Angus appears to have got it into his head that I'm a scoundrel, but Miss McColligan, as I'm sure you ken well, auld Archie McTavish is as pure as a blanket of virgin snow."

He ran his fingers through Lark's tobacco.

"Ha, and the good Dr Latta," he said, speaking more to himself than Lark. "A head full of daft ideas, like others in that profession. If you ask me, a visit to the doctors is a mixture of chance and quackery."

Lark stood, saying nothing.

"Fill you up with arsenic and iron then you're telt to 'take the air', or that vomiting does you good along with slimy little leeches sucking your blood. Eeugh, gives me the jitters," he said with a shiver. "Though at least they dinnae go around sticking their nose into everybody else's business like the church."

Archie lifted the pile of tobacco and transferred it to the scales, glanced up, and let out a gentle laugh. Lark suppressed a gag at the short blast of sour breath.

"Well, Miss McColligan, that's a respectable haul." He looked at her and smiled again. "I'll give you ninepence."

Lark stood open-mouthed. "Ni… ninepence. A… alright, fine."

"And how is your family? I heard your big brother William was up before the magistrates. Aye, serves him right. He cannae seem to stop himself thieving."

"He… he was only in jail for a week."

"Oh, he is a bad lad sometimes, will lead him to no end of trouble. They were lenient this time, next I'm not so sure. They have warned him more than once, I'm telt."

Archie counted two threepenny pieces and three pennies into her hand. "And how's your mother?"

"My maw?" said Lark, somewhat taken aback.

"Yes, how's she managing? Since your poor father Abraham got killed in that altercation with John Preston. We were all good friends when we were youngsters, ya ken."

---

2   *Mutton Shunters (19ᵗʰ cent) – Police.*

"Eh… eh, she's fine." Lark turned and scurried out of the shop back into the lane. *My maw? Ninepence? What on earth was that aboot?*

***

What it was about was that Archie McTavish thought Lark's mother, Mrs Flossie McColligan, a fine-looking woman. Buxom, just the way he liked. While she had dropped a few new members of her brood of thieves and scavengers over the last decades, she still caused his heart to flutter with that lovely auburn hair, those full lips and big, brown, come-to-bed eyes. Now that John Preston had done him the favour of killing her husband, Archie believed her ripe for the picking.

He had never imagined he would get a second chance, but now, he had a plan. Archie and Flossie, together in a pretty little house, away from the town's stink.

He stood and turned to study his reflection. Attempted another squeeze at one boil before a vigorous dig in the right nostril. He stepped back, checking both his left and right profile.

"She doesnae ken it yet, but she is a lucky woman," said Archie to the mirror. "And I've waited a long time."

5. Angus's Awkward Day
Sunday

Superintendent Andrew Angus

Sunday, the Sabbath, the Lord's Day. Superintendent Andrew Angus studied himself in the mirror and caressed his shaved chin. Without a shadow of doubt, his least favourite day of the week. On the other six he worked eighteen hours, and Sundays reminded him why he did. He knew it the only way to keep his sanity.

"Andrew, Andrew!" His wife Bunty's voice came from downstairs. "Hurry, we will be late!"

Angus sighed. "A policeman's lot," he said aloud as he plucked a hair escaping from the nostril of his misshapen nose, "is not always a happy one."

Then, off to church. They stepped out from their home on Water Lane. His uniform tunic sat well on his squat frame. As head of the household, he led from the front, shoulders back, chin up and erect. A step behind, his large wife, Bunty, five inches taller and near the same length wide, with a figure lumpy rather than voluptuous.

Following on were his nine newly scrubbed daughters in a chattering gaggle, trotting to keep up with him as his bandy legs bowled along at the same steady pace as when out patrolling the streets. Both mother and daughters were clad in the same billowing green cotton print frock, the girl's new grey bonnets each with a big halo-shaped brim, the puffy, sagging features of his wife shaded with a similar one in a faded blue.

"And," Bunty's voice grated in his ear, "I need to buy them new petticoats. I want the money by the middle of the week."

"Yes, darling."

"And coal, there's never adequate. My girls complain of the chill and prices are rising all the time. I'll require more housekeeping."

"Mmmm."

"And shoes. Jemimah's are now worn out. You can't expect our daughters to go without shoes."

"Yes, my beloved."

"The butcher and baker's bill; the girls are growing so fast they consume piles of food each week. Paying is the problem. And look at my hat! I'm embarrassed, embarrassed at kirk with it. People will think we are paupers."

Angus was always glad when they reached the top of Kirkgate and passed the columns of Trinity House before turning to enter the imposing arches of South Leith Church. He led them to their mid-priced pew, through the scent of old wood, musty hymn books, perfume and hair oil. He nodded to the others nearby: Corporation of Weavers head man in seats behind, Chairman of the Maltmen to the right, Fleshers' Fraternity secretary to the left.

The wizened, ancient Right Reverend Donald McIntosh in oversized black robes took an age shuffling along the aisle. He appeared to get lost sometimes and zig-zagged his way to the pulpit before struggling to hoist his aged frame up the podium steps.

"Mathew chapter one tells us," he called in a slow, though surprisingly loud, croaky drone, "that Josias begat Jechonias and his brethren, about the time they were carried away to Babylon."

Angus's eyes narrowed

"And after they were brought to Babylon, Jechonias begat Salathiel; and Salathiel begat Zorobabel."

They felt heavy.

"And Zorobabel begat Abiud; and Abiud begat Eliakim."

Superintendent Angus yawned and closed his eyes.

"And Eliakim begat Azor."

Though not in prayer.

A half hour later he woke to rustling hymn books and tuneless singing, bellows wheezed and croaked. He felt rested after his nap, needed the energy. With two unresolved murders in the past fortnight, along with the constant thefts, he had enough on his plate.

At the service end, he herded his daughters out the door, glad to leave before anyone came and plagued him with their list of grievances.

Home to Water Lane for lunch and his one and only weekly gathering with the entire family. Today, Bunty had prepared a joint of mutton, potatoes and gravy. During the week, Angus ate down at the police offices in the new town hall on Charlotte Street, so was able to avoid the usual offerings of overcooked offal, be it liver, tripe or sheep's heart, that Bunty served on weekdays.

Once he had cleared his plate, the afternoon dragged with his wife's constant nipping and all that gossiping, followed by a period of wailing, girning and caterwauling from the girls because Bunty said they couldn't have a pet. After an hour, he excused himself and escaped back to work for the afternoon, keen to hear reports from the patrols around the streets and docks hunting the Sabbath breakers. There were always some, no matter the weather.

Inebriated sailors singing, youths using profanities in the street, working girls working, drunks drinking; a few lads even had the audacity to wheel their barrows with something to sell. His constables marched them to their rooms in the town hall, where he would deal with them once darkness fell, the unwritten rule being that the Kirk Session were happy if he apprehended around a dozen. It seldom took long to nab them. Sometimes Angus joined a patrol himself, and occasionally he hit lucky and apprehended someone who had money and might work out 'an arrangement'.

Some of the Bible-thumpers complained that Sabbath breaking was a severe crime and it was absurd that offenders were no longer able to be whipped in the street, yet others more amiable suggested an extra prayer or two punishment enough.

The problem, of course, was that the rules were not clear. Decrees for keeping the Sabbath for the Congregationalists or Presbyterians were different from customs followed by the Evangelicals. The Evangelicals, of course, didn't agree with the Moderates and certainly not the Calvinists, and there wasn't a chance in hell the Calvinists or the Catholics were ever going to concur with Episcopalians.

And now the added problem of the Floating Chapple in that ancient hulk belonging to the Seamen's Friendly Society in the old East Dock. It teemed with hundreds of destitute urchins on a Sunday afternoon. Fine and well until their service ended, then hordes of them spilled out and started causing all kinds of mischief.

Darkness fell, the lamplighter stopping at each streetlamp with his long pole, the lanterns flicking to life as he progressed along Constitution Street. Superintendent Angus's rule was that with darkness the Sabbath was over, so it was legitimate to go deal with the rabble the magistrate convicted at the Saturday courts. He strode to the Town Hall main entrance and down to the police station in the basement. They kept the stool in an alcove of a room near the cells.

On entering, he adjusted the binding on the rods that had been soaking for the past twenty-four hours and then twisted them together and tied them tight.

Constable Ross brought the first. Angus still had authority to use the stocks and pillory, though they were frowned upon nowadays. Angus considered the punishment kinder when performed in this manner—get it over and done with, then send them on their way. The constables or sergeants could do it if he chose, but he found he enjoyed the exercise.

Constable Ross dragged in the trembling, scrawny boy—grubby, barefoot with scabs on his legs—pulled off his ragged breeches and tied him to the contraption.

"Thieving, third offence," announced the constable.

Angus picked up the birch twigs and took a few practice swings.

There was something satisfying about this. An excellent workout, but it was more than that. Enjoyable though it was, he had always believed a certain aspect missing. He had recently discovered what that was, and better still, he now knew of somewhere to do something about it. The challenge was to meet the expense, then it could be a regular, rather than an occasional treat. He could almost taste it, salivated at the prospect.

"The magistrate ordered six strokes."

Angus turned and eyed the boy tied to the stool.

"Carry on this way, my lad, and you'll end up in the hoose of correction."

"Oh aye, and also whistling on Bernard Street on the Sabbath," said the constable.

Angus gave the youth a stern look and shook his head. "Well, in that case, let's make it seven."

He adjusted his stance and swung his muscled arm with a firm, steady rhythm.

6. The Neighbourhood
Monday

Lark McColligan

Stepping into the courtyard on her way to the Brickwork Close pipe, over her shoulder a long leather water carrier, Lark sang.

"Sweet are the banks—the banks o' Doon,
The spreading flowers are fair,
And everything is blythe and glad,
But I am fu' o' care."

"Whit are you so happy aboot?" interrupted Grannie O'Malley, squatting on the lower steps of Cherry Tree House and resembling a bag of bones in a grubby sackcloth smock, her narrow mouth exposing her two teeth. "If you're so fu' o' care, then have you any baccy for a penniless auld woman?" Grannie O'Malley tightened her shawl over her brow, hacked, then spat.

"Not today," said Lark. "I've no been oot; was helping Maw."

"So," said Tin Pan Aggie (being so called as, apparently, she had never been the same since in her youth she once spent an entire week with an iron pot stuck on her head), dressed in a stained loose-fitting gown of coarse faded cloth, limbs like birch twigs, hatchet face all burst veins and the colour of grubby chalk, "Miss La De Da back again to sit aboot and do nowt, I suppose. Huh, alright for some."

Refusing to take the bait from Aggie's jibe, Lark ignored the pair of old women and crossed the courtyard. Perching on a sill at the corner, she held her face up to a pale sun, and took deep breaths.

The courtyard was off Vinegar Close. Ninety-seven families resided on three sides in cramped tumbledown tenements. A jumble of abodes. Often single ends or two rooms back-to-back, others one over the other. All sharing filthy, crowded earth closets built over rarely emptied cesspits. The communal yard was muddy and unpaved with defective drains, its only open sewer comprising a foul ditch.

As long as she could remember, Lark's maw had told her she was pretty, beautiful even, but, then, that's what maws often do. In reality, she had been a scrawny wee girl, always smaller than her brothers. With siblings, of course, it didn't matter how you looked; all families fought and quarrelled.

Even though she'd lived there most of her life, she'd only lately come to realise that the cherry trees that had given Cherry Tree House its name must be long gone. The house stood on the east side of the courtyard, much older than the rest, from the time of the Stewarts, maybe even Jacobean, with curved, sweeping steps, at the bottom of which groups of women often sat and gossiped. Today, they raised their voices over the din. Banging and hammering came from within as the drawing room was further subdivided.

Cherry Tree House had once been a very grand affair, sturdy and erected on three floors of sandstone, unlike the jerry-built structures with damp, cheap, flaking bricks that now swelled around it. Originally positioned for open views on the edge of town, though long abandoned by the original owners, the family of an affluent merchant who made his fortune through wine and slaves, it was fitted with servants' rooms in the attic and a vast basement kitchen.

When the merchant's family moved on, tradesmen, clerks and overseers had replaced them. Then, from that period of semi-respectability to the present, multiple small rooms had been created out of the formerly elegant dining room and parlours with flimsy partitions linked by dim, windowless corridors and sharing of water and privies. The attics and basements were supplemented by a labyrinth of shanty huts at the rear with dark passages and narrow muddy paths on the former fine gardens and yard where the cherry trees once blossomed.

In place of the one family in occupation, now several poor families shared every corner. Overcrowded and occupied by 143 people, crammed between the cellar and garret roof. A mix of Highland and Irish immigrants, beggars, tramps, thieves, squatters and lowly street girls, who, with few exceptions, lived a life of hunger, chill and thin, scanty attire.

The collection of poor now lived amid the crumbling grandeur of the décor of the former wealthy residents. Intricate stone carvings of angelic cherubs out of place among the half ruins; stains of damp, yellowed, cracked plaster, blotches on the walls; a former fine staircase with broken handrails and rickety stairs. Once beautiful cornices were either missing or stained with mould, neat brass plates which had announced family names now tarnished, along with cladding-stripped sunlit rooms where once were taught drawing, painting and the pianoforte.

While the house appeared unchanging, Lark now noticed other things altered. Over the last year, a sudden blossoming. She had grown taller, with wider hips and real breasts, and that transformed everything. Her relationships with the other young woman round Vinegar Close had turned. She sensed it, judged a few hated her for no reason she understood. She would make quick turns and glance at their secret huddles, the whispers behind her back, never to her face. Sometimes they excluded her. She'd always been included in the past, now less often. Yet with boys, it was the opposite. With increasing regularity, they hovered around her, and new ones kept popping up all the time, full of either bravado or blushes.

Of late, Lark had plenty of suitors among the local young men, also a growing list of chimney sweeps, butchers' lads, bone collectors, barrow boys and trade apprentices. Even drunken sailors calling in the street. Being a member of the McColligan family gave her certain advantages, in that it helped keep the majority at a suitable distance. In one or two cases, William and his band had found an excuse to batter them before they offered her the chance to determine whether she liked them or not.

If these young fellows ever debated the details, they would acknowledge it was because of that flaming mane. Or possibly the understated pout on her lips, that perfect arc of her neck, the smile that could light a gloomy room, her feline movements, or maybe because there was none of that blushing or giggling as with other girls her age. In their deliberations they would have agreed she was unlike any other girl ever encountered, certainly not around Vinegar Close or Yardheads.

Lark had no control over whatever attracted boys to her. After it drew in these young men, she was confident in telling them the facts to their face. She didn't have any problems convincing them they were unsuited, often with only a few words and a haughty glance, but these were defences. She just wasn't ready for that yet. Life was hard enough without adding complications. Lark was aware of the changes, but still undecided about what she was growing to become.

She was straight to the point when any suitor pushed his luck.

"Too stupid," she explained to one.

"Too ugly," she told more than one.

Increasing attentions from the lumbering Big Zander McFarlane were becoming an issue, though, and her brother William looked to encourage it.

"Should keep it in the family," he said.

Big Zander had started to take liberties with his grabbing and groping, all slobbery mouth and muscle with a brain the size of a pigeon's. She'd tried sitting him down and explaining. Expressed with clarity that he was too stupid, too ugly and also a little too rancid, but it hadn't gone in; he just smiled his foolish grin. She'd even punched him on the snout as hard as possible, but her fist only bounced off. He'd laughed, before another clumsy lunge that she needed to be nimble to avoid.

It was all so confusing, a life full of things she didn't yet understand and couldn't control. Could she ever?

7. The Young Reverend Makes Himself at Home
Tuesday

Reverend Allan Ponsonby

Sour faced and drab, Deacon Johnston was late. Young reverend Allan Ponsonby waited at the door.

"Sorry, sorry," spluttered Johnston, his brisk step squelching up the sodden track across the field. "Was tidying up business from yesterday relating to another of the parish properties."

He pulled a rusted key from his pocket.

"Well, here it is."

Deacon Johnston, stick thin, nostrils permanently red and chapped, wiped the continuous drip from his nose before turning the key in the lock. He strained; the stiff door gave way. A puff of dust and old feathers billowed into the air.

"People don't notice this place tucked away here, unused for years. Basic, but the best we can do."

The narrow frame of young Ponsonby stepped over the threshold, features sharp, expression neutral, excitement rising.

The little cottage sat half a mile out of town. They had followed the road westwards out from Sherriff Brae and passed through the field towards the mills before dropping to the narrow, winding path that sloped to the river. The old lodge snuggled in a dip near the water's edge. Two rooms with damp walls and bare floorboards. The front room contained a table and a pair of ancient broken chairs in the corner, two grimy windows and a substantial brick hearth. The spartan back room had one small window and a big empty cupboard with cobwebs and an aged key in the lock.

"I'm sure we can make it habitable," said Ponsonby. "My needs are modest."

He rummaged around in his bag on the floor and drew out a simple wooden cross, stepped forward and placed it above the hearth.

"Used to belong to Borthwick's sawmill further up the river," said the Deacon. "Can recall South Leith bought it a while back, a job lot with a few other properties."

"It's ideal, absolutely ideal. I know already that this is a place where I will find the solitude required for communing with our Lord. I can have the silence that draws me closer to his word. With inner peace, I may know him and he will guide me."

"Yes, quite," said the Deacon, bemused.

Soon after his arrival, the young reverend had made clear to Johnston that he would prefer to lodge somewhere that offered opportunities for solitary contemplation. "The power of worship is stronger when in a peaceful environment."

They stepped into the bedroom, the floor on one side covered in bird droppings, on the other a drip from a hole in the thatch.

"I live through prayer, Deacon Johnston. I'm a follower of Calvin, who instructs us to assign specific hours for that essential purpose each day. As the church's senior deacon, I recommend you do the same." A smirk on his boyish face revealed crooked teeth that appeared to crowd a narrow mouth.

"Quite," sniffed Johnston.

"Observe that guidance and your mind will fill with the word of our Lord. The last time I spoke to him, he told me how I must live."

Deacon Johnston wiped the nasal drip on his sleeve and moved away. Ponsonby followed, standing a touch too close. The Deacon's red nostrils twitched at his putrid breath.

"I pray when I rise in the dawn," said Ponsonby with enthusiasm. "And before I commence daily toil, then when I sit for food, and when with God's grace, I have partaken in it. Finally, at the end of each day, when I retire to rest."

The Deacon kicked the dried bird droppings, scattering feathers and dirt. "I'll arrange someone to mend that hole in the thatch, then tidy up a bit. I can organise a bed and new chairs."

"Ah, thanks. Oh, and a wide bed if possible—I have disturbed sleep."

"Unlikely a problem; we have one in the stores."

"Perfect," said Ponsonby. "Just perfect. I can tell you I feel an affinity towards this place. I can do good works here." He turned and surprised the Deacon with a high-pitched giggle. "My good works, as Luther himself asserted, practices that would please his father, rile the Pope, cause the angels to laugh, and the devils to weep."

The Deacon gave a weak smile.

Just perfect, thought Ponsonby. *Isolated. No prying eyes.*

8. We Meet Important Men
Wednesday

The Kirk Session

The Kirk Session met on the second Wednesday of the month.

Young Reverend Ponsonby arrived early. Footsteps rang on bare floorboards as he stepped into the cavernous meeting chamber. As a mere junior minister, he was honoured they'd requested him prepare the room and take minutes. Keen to impress, he had worn his finest suit (only marginally less threadbare than the other) shaved a wispy chin and combed his thinning hair to the side. He devoted time to planning the layout of table and benches, pondering whether by the stained-glass window or door was best.

Next to arrive, his superior. A nod from the aged minister of the parish. Old Right Reverend Donald McIntosh creaked as he sank a skinny frame into the chairman's cushioned seat. The chair creaked, too.

Moments later, the squat, potbellied Mr Alexander Preston, representative from Leith Bank and financial adviser to the Kirk, arrived, accompanied by the severe face and sagging jowls of Mr Adam White, a Baltic trader with stakes in banking and shipping. Heavy, pear-shaped and dressed in a long fawn coat with black velvet lapels and a white cravat at the throat, he forced his great behind into his chair. Mr White, presently also the Police Commissioner, would shortly be installed as Leith's first ever Provost. Next year, the town would become a separate municipal burgh with its own magistrates and council and at last gain independence from Edinburgh after hundreds of years' servitude.

Following close behind him came a gaggle of a dozen black suits of the elders and deacons that completed the Kirk Session, soon arranged on benches around the large table of the spartan hall. Last to appear was the gaunt, lanky, red-nosed Lord Haddington. On his lips an aristocratic sneer and narrow-faced frown, framed by bushy whiskers.

More flamboyantly dressed than the rest, with a top hat and quality long black coat with a wide shaped collar. He bared the points of his teeth with a sly, lopsided smile, then sat.

Bringing his gavel down with a smack, old Reverend McIntosh called the session to order. "Elders of the Kirk. Gentlemen, for today's meeting we will follow the usual agenda and start with the beggars before moving to dealing with the rest."

Lord Haddington stood up, struck the table with his fist and bellowed, "The undeserving poor. Now, gentlemen, if you recall we left our last meeting with a dilemma to ponder." His drooping features a picture of scorn, he spluttered, "Pah, there're hordes of them, more appearing each day. God-fearing people can't stroll through the streets of Leith without being accosted by some sturdy-looking beggar. Today, ragged urchins approached me more than once, trying to browbeat me into giving. Had to take my cane to them. There is no escape, they cluster into every ally, loitering on every street demanding alms."

"It's the fault of Edinburgh. They had a clear out a week past and they have moved here," said Johnston, the sour senior deacon. He wiped the perpetual drip falling from his thin nose.

Haddington's face reddened. He thumped the table again. "It's a disgrace, and something has to be done."

Commissioner White laid his elbows on the table and gave a long sigh. He brought his fingers together below his chin and spoke.

"What His Lordship has to understand is that the country is changing. The expanding modern industry is drawing people from the countryside. They worked the land in days past, but now one threshing machine produces the work of thirty men."

"Pah," said Haddington, who sat with folded arms.

"What we have to accept," said White, "is that whether they are our own beggars, or whether it's the impoverished Irish, Highlanders, or Jews, and whatever they are running from, be it famine or persecution, it makes no difference. They have no option but to pour into towns searching for work. It's happening over the entire country."

"Work," exclaimed Haddington. "We are the individuals who do the work—us, industrialists, shipbuilders, landowners, the church. We are the ones who created the industries, the paper and textile mills, print shops and ropeworks. That scum just hangs around all day, making trouble for the town's tradespeople as well as ourselves." He jabbed the table with his finger. "And persecuted? Perhaps the answer is that we should persecute them by transporting the lot of them to Australia along with the other criminals."

Young Ponsonby winced, the tendons in his hand straining, scribbling fast to record the grumbles and comments that now swirled around the table.

"Gentlemen, gentlemen," said Mr Preston[3], the banker raising his palms to calm the dispute. "Can we please recognise that these problems are outside the remit of the Kirk Session? Our role is to distribute funds for those poor unfortunates who, through sickness and misfortune, are entitled to a little relief from the parish."

"Agreed," said Lord Haddington. "Rather than waste energy discussing the ideas of those who might encourage bitterness and revolt—though I'd wager these modernisers are most bitter about their own lack of worldly goods in comparison to others." He glared at Mr White.

Mr Preston lifted a paper from the table. "I quote: the aged poor, impotent and decayed persons who must by necessity live by alms."

To look at him, given the quality of his fine woollen suit, it was difficult to believe, but Mr Preston understood the poor. He remembered where he came from, long ago, not much more than a stone's throw from where they now sat. Nobody would recognise him from childhood, and it was something he was keen to keep a secret and never to advertise.

"Or, to put it another way," said Haddington. "The sick, invalid, cripples, halfwits, foundlings and riff-raff who infest the town."

"As you all know, gentlemen," said Preston, ignoring the comment, "the strategy we have works well. What is collected in the poor box each Sunday is then distributed to our own deserving needy. We issue them a badge so locals know to whom to give and whom to ignore."

"But the poor box is near empty," said Deacon Johnston.

"It does appear that when need is the greatest, funds are the lowest," said Commissioner White, sounding perplexed.

"Cut the pensions we offer in half, I suggest," said Haddington. "The new extension to my mill will be ready soon. We can take on more employees; that will help mop up a few."

Mr Preston sighed a sorrowful sigh. When he was a child, his father had gone back to sea after his mother died. It had left him the choice of following him or else trying to survive among the other scavengers

---

3   *Banker Alexander Preston appears in chapters 15 and 16 of* Leithers – One Family.

and vagrants of Leith. He had chosen the ocean and pursued his father out to the Caribbean. Then came jobs and relationships he didn't really want to remember, personal sadness, lost loves and professional failure until he arrived at the Leith Bank and everything changed for the better.

"The tremendous increase in the population has resulted in severe problems of overcrowding, malnutrition and epidemics. We just don't have the infrastructure," said Mr White. "You can almost taste the hardship; we need to improve their conditions."

"But that doesn't solve the problem," said Lord Haddington. "Have you seen the hordes of destitute children around the docks? They are nothing but a pest, like rodents." He rapped on the table.

Commissioner White interjected. "Fact is labouring men in the harbour depend on the dawn call for work at the dock gates, and that depends on wind and season. Their casual and irregular jobs often come together or not at all. It's always been thus. As a result, families of these children face economic insecurity."

"The aim of the investor is to make money, plain and simple," said Haddington. He stood again to force his point. "Our aim is economic growth, so what we require is an efficient port to allow us to trade what we produce, and these hordes of poor are affecting our efficiency."

"But who is responsible for them?" said Deacon Johnston, his tone peevish. "A rapid and unplanned influx into the towns was always going to cause immense problems, put enormous pressures on accommodation and everything else. We did not design the poor law and religious institutions such as our own to grapple with such explosive urban growth."

"Well," said Lord Haddington, "it's not our problem unless they work for us. The ancient trade corporations, be it mariners, carters or shoemakers, do the same. They look after their own, nobody else."

"Yes." Mr White's jowls wobbled as he raised his voice further. "The issue is that unlike the ancient trade fraternities, you factory owners don't take responsibility for your own workers. It's a degradation that you have children working sixteen hours a day in your mills and factories, and for a mere pittance."

Lord Haddington looked indignant. "How dare you, sir, and what on earth is wrong with that? The sole advantage I have encountered in having these unwelcome masses of poor is that it has helped drive wages lower."

The young Reverend Ponsonby raised his hand. "You will be glad to know that our church has now held special services for the

underprivileged youngsters, in the floating chapel by the old dock."
He smiled ingratiatingly. "We already have impressive numbers. I'm
sure it can improve things and ease the problem."

His lordship looked bemused. "Quite."

The Right Reverend McIntosh in the chair lifted his eyes above
his spectacles, making his first and only contribution to the discussion.
"Most praiseworthy."

Lord Haddington's florid features reddened further. "And," he
said, stabbing a finger firmly on the table, "some of you here no doubt
support the ludicrous Reform Act being brought in this year, and
where will that end? Power in the land should stay with the owners of
the land. These reform proposals suggest a full thirteen percent of the
men in the country can vote in future. It's outrageous. I fear where it
will lead, some kind of revolution most likely, as happened in France.
Who are you allowing to vote next? The tradesmen? Or how about
beggars?" he said with a mocking laugh.

Commissioner White stared back, indignant. "We need to get
reform done."

"And then what?" roared Haddington. "Women voting, I suppose,
or shoeless urchins. How about horses?"

"Now you're just being ridiculous," said White, turning away.

"I agree," piped up Deacon Johnston. "It's gone on far too long.
We just need to get reform done. And once Leith gets its own town
council next year, with Mr White as our new Provost, we might have
the power to do something with the terrible housing, maybe even clear
the slums and shanties."

Mr White nodded, a half-smile crossing his grey features. "The
new Reform Act is a major step forward and will aid both local
and national governance of the country. A whole range of modern
developments and lots of things will improve, including housing for
the poor if we get the resources. My intention is to run the town
differently, no longer under Edinburgh's yoke. Time for a new model
of business. If we can attract new investment, then everybody benefits,
even the beggars."

Haddington leapt to his feet once again. "I fear what these reforms
might bring," he growled. "These sweeping, ill-considered changes.
Also, the farce that slavery is being abolished throughout the entire
empire next year, an outrageous assault on our past freedoms."

"Freedom," exclaimed White, his jaw dropping. He tried to rise
but found that because of his massive rump he was now stuck in his

chair, so abandoned the idea with a grunt. "So, slavery is freedom now, is it?"

"Of course, it is—that's exactly what's lost," said Haddington. "The white man's mastery over these lesser races meant that rather than live under the control of some local black despot, they were educated to enable them to live as Christians."

"But the chains and shackles," said White, looking incredulous. "What of them?"

"And didn't Jesus suffer for our sins?" shot back Haddington. "You reformers will be the end of us all."

Haddington fell back into his seat with a grunt of exasperation. White responded with a hard stare through tight lips, both still fencing with their eyes.

Seeing the opportunity, Alexander Preston jumped to his feet. "The accounts."

Then, to justify his fee, for the next fifteen minutes he droned on about assets and accruals, cash and credit, then liabilities and liquidity, confirming in his summing up that the Kirk Session's poor box had little more than two brass farthings to rub together.

Mr Preston had much for which he was thankful. By pure luck, he'd found himself at Leith Bank, the right place at the right time, just as the seaport had boomed, creating great opportunities and benefits.

On completion of his financial report, he gathered his notes.

"And now." Old Reverend McIntosh brought down his gavel. "Now, gentlemen, the next item on the agenda." He shuffled his papers. "The fornicators."

Disapproving grumbles swept around the table. Alexander Preston rose and made his goodbyes, no doubt glad to return to work away from these squabbles. He did not require reminding of the poor, or any part of his life before the bank. That was best forgotten.

9. The Superintendent Makes a Discovery
Thursday

Superintendent Andrew Angus

There was a time when the Pig and Bell Tavern stood alone on the road out of town. Now there was no one living who could remember when it sat apart. It was built from sturdy ship beams taken from wrecks hundreds of years earlier; narrow, crooked and weather-beaten timbers huddled and leaning between the scruffy tumbledown stone houses that had grown around it in Brickwork Close.

In a stiff breeze, it might creak as a ship in a light swell, as locals came and went, a constant stream of housewives, sailors' destitute children, dogs, horses and carts tramping along the muddy lane and past its doors. A midden next door and its long-established leaching cesspit gave it the local nickname, the Stinking Pig.

The basement stank, a fug of stale tobacco, sweat, the middens and ale, with another unfamiliar scent.

"What's that smell?" asked Superintendent Angus.

"Dried blood," said Mr Roberts, the tavern landlord. "Haven't had time to clean oot last night's rats."

The superintendent's nose wrinkled. "Well, it stinks. It's, it's… an unholy stench, unholy blood."

Roberts appeared to stifle a snicker at Angus's words before Angus realised it was actually a cough.

They stooped to pass through a low door into the narrow back lane, where a pair of booted legs were sticking out a drain. Another one, just like the others. Superintendent Angus knew before the body was lifted.

He nodded to his men. With Constable McDonald a full two feet taller than Constable Ross, it was awkward. They took a leg each and pulled, then grabbed the belt and hefted the dead weight out of the duct, sending it sprawling onto the cobbles.

The man wore fawn breeches and a dark, short jacket, his knee-length riding boots flecked with grime. A fellow of imposing height, lean and muscular, with thick, congealed sewage clinging to his upper body.

"Get a bucket," ordered Angus.

Constable McDonald retreated to the cellar, and returned, bucket filled.

"Let's see who we've got." McDonald emptied the pail in the man's face.

Narrow jawed with a thin beard. Maybe early forties, glassy eyes still open in a leathery face. Angus turned to Roberts, who shook his head.

"Dinnae recognise him. Came this morning, opened basement door to clear the air, and here he was."

Superintendent Angus bent and studied. There, the tell-tale signs: black blotches on the neck, a thin crust of dried blood around the mouth. This, the third body in a month, each murdered. Each, it appeared, by this same method.

"Likely, the poor fellow staggered into the lane in his death throes before ending in the drain."

"Might have been a lovers' tiff," said Constable Ross. "Or jealous boyfriend wha's girlfriend was being pestered."

Angus snorted. "Oh, I see. 'I love you. Would you like me to kill someone for you?'"

"Might have fallen oot with yin of his pals," said Constable McDonald.

"Don't be stupid," snapped Angus. "He's been poisoned, and this has got gang killing all over it. No, I know him." He bared his teeth in frustration.

Only two days before, Angus had sat in this man's office surrounded by stacks of contracts, wills and deeds of sale. Together, they'd been investigating discrepancies discovered in several legal documents affecting important trade transactions. The lawyer had informed Angus that a pattern was emerging and he was getting close to discovering who might be behind it. But now this.

"It's a professional job, clear this man crossed someone and now's payback, same as the others. He had a lawyer's office just down the road in Riddle's Close. Was one of my informers."

"But whit gang?" said Ross.

"Well, that's the bloody problem we are trying to solve," snapped Angus. "We don't have the slightest clue who. This wave of crime in the port, these killings, they are not random. Obvious they're victims of the same mob. Question is who, and how to unmask them."

Mr Roberts' sly eyes peered at the floor.

"I could go undercover," said Constable McDonald. "See if I might infiltrate them."

"Same here," said Ross. "I'd be better at it, so pick me, choose me."

Angus turned and looked them hard in the eye. "Did either of you go to school?"

McDonald nodded.

"I've got nothing against education—as long as it doesn't interfere with your reasoning. So, tell me your theory."

"Eh... Um... Err..."

"I need to get the body oot the lane," interrupted Roberts. "We have another ratting tonight. Dead bodies lying around the place will put customers off. I've the Stinking Pig's reputation to protect. The place needs cleaned up."

Angus frowned.

"Alright, lads, the cart's outside, remove the body."

"Wha's next in line, I wonder," said Constable McDonald as they struggled to lift the dead weight back through the door up the narrow stairs.

Angus noted Roberts' anxious eyes. He turned to him. "Don't worry, Mr Roberts, we have discovered these bodies in the most unlikely of places, so I don't believe you're in any danger despite him being found outside your basement."

The policemen unceremoniously dragged the dead man out the front door and heaved him onto the cart.

That afternoon, Angus visited the murdered lawyer's premises. He questioned his housekeeper, who'd seen nothing untoward the day before, but when she had arrived that morning, the door was unlocked and the bed not slept in. She'd also been surprised to find a table set for two in his private apartment, all the trimmings with candles and fine crockery but the food on the plates untouched. She could make no sense of it, and neither could the superintendent.

10. Charlie's Epiphany
Friday

Charlie Preston

What could it be?

Charlie Preston thrust his hands into the icy mud once again. Wriggling his fingers, he closed his palms, forming a firm grip around the solid shape. Numb with cold. It was long thin and smooth. He pulled hard and felt it move an inch. And again, another inch.

His hands were raw, as if his fingers were about to drop off. He withdrew them, rubbed them together, tried to blow in a little heat.

"Tommy, Tommy, I've got something but I cannae get it oot."

Leaving the decrepit smack he was working under, his older brother staggered through the mire, a familiar determined expression on his florid wide face. Naked blue feet lifted high with each step. His ragged, wet black cloak was mud spattered.

"Whit have you got?"

"I dinnae ken. It's heavy, long and smooth, possible a nice bit iron, could be an auld windlass bar, or maybe an ancient blade."

Together, they thrust their hands back in, wrapped them around the object, yanked hard. It shifted again. They tugged and pulled. Each time it moved an inch, a whiff of oily stink burst from rising bubbles as air escaped from the space they created beneath it. After a few minutes, they both stood, blowing with the effort. Charlie glanced up and saw their audience, sitting on the Shore bollards, the McColligans. Wee Andy and William with his sidekick Big Zander and, standing behind, Lark.

"Whit have you got Preston?" called William with a grin. "A Mermaid?"

"Bugger off, McColligan," snarled Tommy.

Ignoring them, the Preston boys thrust their hands back in the icy slime. After a minute, the object shifted, moved a bit more.

"Dig deep!" shouted Tommy, strain on his ruddy features.

Suddenly, the mud's resistance broke. It was free at last. Their faces fell as a long thin piece of smooth rock split the water's surface.

"Shit!" cried Tommy, dropping it back in, just missing Charlie's foot.

"Watch it," squealed Charlie.

"Ha ha," shouted William from the quayside before he stood and moved off, laughing.

"Stuff this," said Charlie. "I've had it with working the mud. I want something new."

"Don't talk daft," said Tommy, frowning. "Oor folk have always been mudders. Oor maw used to be, as was oor dad before he got killed. Whit else would you do anyways?"

"Look," replied Charlie, exasperated. "There's nothing happens in this game apart from getting your hands and feet frozen aff. Aye, or sailors pissing over the rail of their ship on your head. I want a better life. I'm done with it."

Freezing water swirled around their legs as the tide flooded. They battled their way through the sludge and approached the bottom of the ladder.

"There loads of things I might do—chimney sweeping."

"Whit? No chance. You're too big, wouldn't get up the chimney."

"A barrow laddie—become a costermonger, selling stuff."

"Selling whit?" said Tommy with a scornful glance. "We might supply wee scraps of coal and bent nails, and you have to afford a barrow first."

Charlie frowned. "Selling stuff for Fat Archie from his scrap shop," he suggested. "Bootlaces, rags."

"Whit, work with that old crook? I'm sure you will end up rich."

"Employed as a porter on the wharf."

"No chance," scoffed Tommy. "You would have to be a member of their corporation, and that doesn't happen unless your father was before you."

"A carter."

"Carters' Society, Corporation of Weavers, Fraternity of Mariners—the clue's in the name. No for the likes of you. We are the bottom of the pile." Tommy looked thoughtful for a moment. "Well, apart from the shit shovellers that do the cesspools."

"Rat catcher."

"You need dogs and then train them for years," said Tommy, mocking. "Anyway, once you start working the street, would have the McColligans to contend with.

"Your choices are: this"—Tommy pointed at the mud—"or else beggar, or a thief and end up in jail, or worse. Or sail oot to sea, if a sailor's life for you, fine, good luck. Of course, there's the glassworks, mills and rope factory, that's if lucky enough to find employment, and you ken whit that does. At least with this, you're likely to keep your fingers and toes. Or else join oor maw in the dust yard working that ash sieve all day."

Charlie frowned and looked up, noticed Lark still sitting on the bollard leaning over the quay. She hadn't moved off with her brothers and Zander. He couldn't stop himself staring. Was something graceful about her, those exquisite features and fine shape. Was gratifying.

"Whit are you gawking at?" said Tommy with an expression of incredulity. "And aye, she has grown up quite a bit of late, but dinnae even think it." His eyes tightened as an intense frown crossed his face. "The lassie's a McColligan."

Charlie glanced again just as a slender ray of sun split the blanket of dark cloud and lit the head of flaming red hair. It resembled the golden halo in the pictures Charlie saw in the books at the Floating Chapple. Lark returned his stare and didn't look away. She was taller than he remembered. Charlie didn't know why, but he found himself smiling. She didn't smile back.

His toes touched something hard, and he bent to draw out an old winch handle. When he raised his eyes again, she was gone.

11. The Neighbours
Saturday

Flossie McColligan

Would she ever want another man?

Flossie hoisted the pile of washing onto the wall at the steps and nodded to the other women. There were few decent men around, and she had noted Fat Archie McTavish popping up more regularly, all smiles. She didn't think so; she wasn't that desperate. Not yet anyway.

While scrubbing at the Brickwork Lane standpipe, she had been thinking of the all the men in her life. The sweet memory of her first love, a local lad now gone. She had loved him twice over. Her father—he was a brute and best forgotten. Her husband had started as a decent man before his descent into the drink. All those years wasted with the drunken Abraham from which she had received nothing. Apart from her children.

As Flossie shook a shirt from her basket, she spotted all five of them on the other side of the yard, leaving together. William at the front, all bluster and swagger in that smart tailcoat and battered hat he always wore. The younger boys, Eck and Wee Andy, looked like smaller versions of their big brother but were a pair of sweeties really. But now, she worried they were starting to follow William's ways. She wished they wouldn't, but what could she do about it? Flossie worried where that might lead in future. William had always been a difficult child. Hopefully one day they would all get proper jobs and be able to settle down.

Coming behind, Lark, slender yet sturdy, with that hair, hand in hand with wee Eliza, a little tomboy with curls and the darkest brown eyes, the pair of them laughing together as always, off to scour the area for baccy.

Flossie pushed back a strand of hair that had escaped from her cap, and grinned. They were hers and she was proud of them all. Some more than others, not that she would ever say that out loud. Lips pinched at the thought, Flossie lifted her basket and joined the other women.

"It's the gypsies, wha else could it be?" said Tin Pan Aggie.

Big Zander's equally big maw, Mrs McFarlane, lifted a plump forearm and clipped the final peg to the line that stretched between the damp bricks of the tenements and the hook on the wall of Cherry Tree House.

"Well, what I do ken is that whoever it is must be a ballyragging[4] devil," she said. "Except that it's no funny."

"Might not be a he, might be a she for all we ken," said Grannie O'Malley.

Tin Pan Aggie's slack jaw tightened. "Dinnae be stupid. It's obvious it's them wha done it. Same as the root of half the crime in the port. Three murders in the space o' a couple o' weeks—I dinnae feel safe in my bed."

A sudden gust raised a billowing cloud of dust, laying a grey film across Mrs McFarlane's sheet. A mirthless smile on Flossie's generous lips, she pulled her last shirt from the basket.

"But the gypsies dinnae come until harvest is over," said Flossie. "I've not seen a single gypsy since last year."

"Wha then?" said Mrs McFarlane.

"Och well," said Aggie. "Eh… eh, likely it's the Irish. They are a right rough lot."

"Naw, naw," said Grannie O'Malley. "Not us. More chance will be the gentry. That Lord Haddington has married three times, and two have died, so I'm telt. I've heard he's a devil worshipper."

"Aye, I'm told as a young laddie he lived in Paris," said Aggie, frowning. "So, a foreigner in oor midst. I can see it: him with his bandy legs, doorknocker[5] puss and smile o' a hungry dug."

Grannie's voice dropped to a whisper. "Normally I wouldn't tell this, I'd keep it hidden." She glanced over both shoulders. "I've picked up all the rumours about him and the other toffs. They say yin o' them was a former priest wha lost his faith and sailed right round the world on every kind of ship as a murderous pirate. I'm telt he was also a kidnapper wha sold slaves."

---

4   *Ballyrag (19th cent) – to bully, esp. through cruel jokes.*
5   *Doorknocker (19th cent) – A type of beard "formed by the cheeks and chin being shaved, leaving a chain of hair under the chin and upon each side of mouth, forming with moustache something like a door-knocker."*

"Naw, naw," said Mrs McFarlane. "That must be another toff. They would never have let Haddington join the Kirk Session if that was all true. Much more likely it's the Catholics or else the Frenchies, or maybe the Jews wha's to blame for all the murders, and you ken whit they did to oor Lord, so why wouldn't they do it again?"

"Naw, cannae be them," said Grannie. "We've only a handful of Hebrews, and they spend every hour sewing. Anyway, I'm told the bodies hadn't been robbed."

"They will be wanting to drink the blood," said Mrs McFarlane, face grim.

"Rubbish," said Flossie. "And if it's not the gentry or gypsies, it's much more likely to be members of the Kirk Session. The Presbyterians. I wouldn't trust that lecherous lot beneath that holier-than-thou front they put on. Bunch of Bible-thumping bastards they are, sticking their nose into anybody's business."

"Well," said Grannie, pulling her shawl tighter around her head. "I've gleaned rumours o' a secret criminal fraternity in the toon that sucks blood as well, sounds unholy by Christ. If it's true that might be these Presbyterians. They are never oot of Madam McPherson's place off Burgess Lane. I've seen them creeping in, but I ken wha they are. They are a shifty lot. You can see it on their pusses."

"I ken wha it was," said Aggie, on her face the smug look of someone suddenly in the know. "Whit's the yin thing that we have far too much o' in this toon of late?"

"Ships."

"Naw."

"Eh… bad weather."

"Naw."

"The French pox."

"Naw."

"Well whit?" said Grannie, exasperated.

"Beggars," said Aggie.

"Aye, yer right enough, Aggie," said Mrs McFarlane. "Aye, o' course, that's wha will be to blame, the murderous devils."

"Aye, the vagrants. The sooner we drive them oot, the better," said Aggie.

"There wouldn't be a body left," said Flossie, mocking. "And that needs to include you as well."

"Harrumph," said Aggie. "Am different, I'm an official beggar. I've got the badge fae the Kirk Session."

Grannie O'Malley's eyes narrowed. She hacked, pulled out her pipe, then spat.

12. Reverend Ponsonby Finds Solace
Sunday

Reverend Allan Ponsonby

"Oh Hosanna," sang the youngsters.

"With hearts full of praise," responded the young reverend.

"Oh Hosanna."

The Reverend Ponsonby sang in reply, "Be exalted, oh Lord my God."

He raised his arms, almost a dance, the well-used hymn book flapping above his head. The sound reverberated around the bowels of the converted old hulk. Its aged timbers creaked in protest as the piano and voices boomed from the cavernous hold. Then, with a final flourish at the top of his voice, "Hosanna in the highest. Glory to the king of kings."

Reverend Ponsonby liked to entertain in his services, to inspire and to be spontaneous. None of that dry, dull, droning in the style of his senior colleague at South Leith.

The ladies who had volunteered to attend from the Religious Tract Society and the Sabbath School at the church had warbled along with the song. They now moved to the bow of the hulk to prepare the meal with benign smiles. Though a few with lime-sour lips, implying their disquiet at Ponsonby's over-exuberance.

However, Ponsonby's aim had never been to impress these good-hearted, tight-lipped ladies. He had limited experience with women other than his mother, who for as long as he could remember, he had despised with venom.

The reverend glanced towards the door in the stern. *He'd better not be late.* Then, turned and peered over the throng of over a hundred destitute waifs. Most ragged and thin, their eyes followed him in expectation. He checked their grubby faces, saw hunger among hollow cheeks and teeth like splinters, the poor little wastrels.

An early memory of mother was the realisation she didn't love him. Soon, it became obvious she didn't want him either. Of his father, a recollection of him at home, but no remembrance of talking with him, not a solitary word. It was as if his parents had mocked him. Then, his mother sent him to a church boarding school where he had not a single friend and a faint recollection of being buggered most nights by the bigger boys.

Back then, it had doused his spirits to be held in such low esteem by other people, despite his efforts to be unfailingly courteous. Now, however, he kept others at a distance by choice rather than necessity. He'd found freedom in avoiding the burdens of responsibility that warm relationships might bring; they only led to recriminations and guilt prompted by the expectations of others.

It was only when he discovered Calvin and the Lord that he was rescued. Things much improved with the creator to guide him. He had seized control of his life, liked the feeling that gave him, and the joy and satisfaction it brought.

Despite his agility, Reverend Ponsonby did not cut an impressive figure. Skinny arms and legs struggled to fill his threadbare black suit. A scrawny chicken neck and bobbing Adam's apple that left a significant gap around his dog collar. Blotchy skin on a wide, boyish face with a long, beaky nose. Thinning hair topped a melon shaped head. When he smiled, thin lips revealed crooked teeth among a weak mouth and chin. But in contrast, his eyes were a striking winter blue, glowing with the fervour of a man on a mission.

The song ended with an inward smile, cheered by the multitude attending his new Sunday service for poor children. What a success. Elders of the parish who initially appeared resistant were now likely impressed with the numbers. His senior, the Reverend McIntosh, agreed the service a positive response to the problem of the destitute youths running wild around the dock area. Plus, his superiors were no doubt happy they might avoid having to give a thought to letting any of this congregation into their church. That would not be popular with the middle-class parishioners who paid a handsome price for pews at South Leith.

The mastless old hulk, rotted in parts, with flaked paint and the inescapable stink of damp, had known better days. But now it was put to good use by the Seamen's Friendly Society, who ran their own services and education groups for sailors and their families at its berth in the East Dock. They'd hired Ponsonby to run a few of their Bible studies classes, as his meagre wage as a junior minister at South Leith meant he struggled to pay for what he needed.

However, at his behest, his superiors now agreed that it was only the poorest who poured into the old hulk on a Sunday afternoon. One of the lower decks had been dismantled, giving added space to the hold to make up the large assembly hall which filled most of the ship.

The Reverend Ponsonby had prepared today's sermon with this audience in mind:

"Mathew chapter nineteen tells us: suffer the little children and forbid them not to come unto me." He looked up towards the roof timbers, passion on his face. "For such is the kingdom of Heaven." Then he paused for dramatic effect. "And soon all you youngsters will receive food from our church to allow you to share in our Lord's abundance, over there at the bow of the ship… a marvellous spread of vegetable soup and white bread served up by the ladies of the parish."

Rows of youths yelled and cheered, fidgeting in anticipation. Ponsonby called for silence for one last song before the bread was broken. The piano tinkled, old wizened Mrs Brown's voice forceful as she played, the children quick to pick up the chorus.

Singing drowned out the creaking door at the ship's stern, but the reverend noticed Fat Archie McTavish as he slipped in through the rear hatch. Ponsonby gave him a barely discernible nod of acknowledgement as the song ended and the volume of expectant babble among the youngsters increased.

Reverend Ponsonby scanned the rows again. These poor children had nothing, their lives blighted by disease and violence. He examined the sad state of their clothes, little more than rags, enough to scare a scarecrow. The few girls at the front closest to him with just thin, scanty coverings and their white knees, upon which he couldn't seem to stop fixing his eyes. And the older ones, the shapes of thighs and breasts bulging under taut rags. But these were for another day. He had already made his choice, the name he would slip to Archie McTavish.

He felt the power of the Lord course through him.

Yes, thought Ponsonby. *Suffer the little children—and bring them to me.*

13. Charlie's Realisation
Monday

Charlie Preston

This morning the tide was high, so Charlie had gone to help Tommy move a load of turnips. Then, in the afternoon, to work with his mum Edith at the dust yard on the links. He found her and his wee sister working near the ropeworks in the space where the piles of residue discarded from thousands of coal fires were collected, the source of the town's permanent smoke columns. Charlie slipped past the queue of horses and dustcarts, the contents of each wagon to be added to the huge blackened conical heap in the centre of a throng of ash-stained women and children.

Charlie found Edith's stocky frame standing firm in a coarse, dirty cotton gown amid a sooty mass of white ash and cinders. Her arms were bared to the elbows, her tired, grime-covered face in a battered bonnet. Around her waist was a heavy leather apron as her hand moved with a steady rhythm, striking the ash-filled sieve against the thick hide.

The accumulation of fine dust she created would be taken by the farms for manure. Charlie helped with shovelling the remaining cinders into baskets; these were added to a different heap for the brickworks. Wee Annie's job was to pick out any old bricks or oyster shells to be lifted to a third pile and sold to road builders.

"You appear distracted, Charlie," said Edith.

"Bet he's been kissing a lassie," laughed wee Annie. "Charlie's always hanging aboot them." She giggled and burst into song: "Charlie and his girlfriend up a tree, k-i-s-s-i-n-g."

"Shut up, Annie." Charlie took a swipe she swerved to avoid.

"Ooh, might have touched a nerve there," said Edith with a fatigued smile.

Of course, Charlie knew wee Annie was right. He was irritated by her constantly mocking his long sequence of girlfriends, yet his longest relationship to date had endured a week. There'd been the one with the irritating, squeaky, high-pitched voice. The big-built, friendly one with bad breath. The whining gin-loving one. The one with the watery eyes and chapped nose who didn't stop talking for a single second.

But this time was going to be different. He had thought of her earlier on his way to the dust yard, spent a sleepless past few nights analysing how she'd gazed at him from the wharf last Friday. Their eyes had met. Then she'd tilted her nose up. He hadn't been able to establish whether the look was of interest or disinterest. Or was it one of offence?

At the Floating Chapple yesterday, he wasn't concerned with the churchman's performance. Was more interested in watching the back of Lark's head from the bench behind. He liked the way she moved. He'd studied the shape of her neck and had considered whether to pluck up the courage to speak to her when outside. And would she reply? With her brother William around, he'd been unsure it was a wise idea.

After his maw's shift ended, they headed home. A stop at the market to spend her earnings on a few pennies' worth of bread, cheese and suet. After the meagre meal, Charlie stepped out, and wandered over the bridge to check the street.

When he spotted it, couldn't believe his luck. A nice cigar down the side of the Custom House. A real cracker, thick and of choicest quality; they could only have taken a few puffs before it dropped. He picked it up, then stumbled backwards in surprise. Lark had popped up right in front of him, as if by magic, a fierce scowl on her lips.

She moved her face to within an inch of his, pointing a finger that touched his chin.

"That's mine," she growled. "I spotted it first." And she snatched the cigar out of his hand before turning and trudging back towards the bridge.

Charlie stumbled sideways, realised he needed to sit on the Custom House steps. A strange force was passing through him. He'd no prior memory of feeling this way. It was all-embracing.

Charlie knew that today was a day he would always remember. Likely a moment to savour the rest of his life. A sensation coursing through his soul. Lightheaded, was he ill? As if something had shifted. The air was fresher, sky brighter, the sound of the rushing river changed—to music.

The Custom House steps were busy as usual with ship skippers coming to declare their cargos jostling with suited clerks dashing in and out. That bustle drifted over him. Charlie fingered his chin where she'd touched him, the spot hot, and then, with her having been so close... Those lips, he could taste them. The bright green eyes, that flame red hair, those freckles, her scent. It took a full three minutes for him to regain his composure, and the realisation hit him; it was wonderful. And that hand she'd used to touch his face, did it only have four fingers, missing a pinkie?

He wished to see her again. In fact, he needed to. Now, it was the most important thing in his life.

The bell of St Ninian's struck five as the evening light faded. He would always recall that chime. But where might they meet? He couldn't risk going near the McColligan's patch, but maybe on the street... His mind turned to next Sunday afternoon. She was bound to be at the Floating Chapple in the old East Dock.

14. Lark Considers Men
Tuesday

Lark McColligan

Under the arches of the entrance to Cant's Ordinary Tavern, amidst the familiar stink of male sweat, beer and tobacco, was always an excellent spot. The group of merchant ship officers laughed and stepped inside. Lark strode forward to pick up three cigar tabs and added them to her sack before returning to her hand cart parked outside Murphy's chandlers.

The hum of Market Day on the Kirkgate. Lark traversed the busy, narrow thoroughfare, pushing the borrowed barrow. Squeaking wheels announced her arrival at the marketplace. Gable-end peaks jutted out above the row of little shops. Bakers and haberdashers, cabinet makers and glove manufacturers. The muddy street was crowded with the usual blend of housewives, children, tradesmen, drunken sailors and both deserving and undeserving beggars.

All kinds of commodities were available from the stands, booths and stalls. From apples to turnips to second-hand horseshoes. A torrent of abuse was aimed at a wagon causing a jam loaded with blocks of cheese and pulled by a stubborn-eyed donkey. A hoot from a river steamer in the distance. Hawkers selling everything from bootlaces to penny pamphlets. The butcher's stall, his red-stained apron and lingering odour of dried blood. Pig trotters lined up in tidy rows, above them strings of raw, plucked chickens. Lark's mouth watered with the aroma of roasting meat from the sheep's head oozing on a spit.

On the other side, children held out grubby little palms for a halfpenny, huddled together at the entrance to a narrow vennel. Their ragged clothes scarcely covered them. Months of dirt clung to skin, one with a hacking cough that shook her chest. These too weak even as factory fodder. One, too pushy, received a whack with a metal-tipped cane from a passing gent.

Further up the street, leaving the gates of Scott's Brewery, were a pair of enormous muscular Clydesdale horses pulling a cart with a great stack of barrels of beer and spirit. Their nostrils flared, belching steam, as the driver goaded them up the gradient with his whip.

Lark took the borrowed barrow with her borrowed stock and set up between a girl with nimble fingers laying out prunes and an old man on a stool making wicker baskets with experienced hands.

Lark emptied her cart of its contents and turned it upside down. Barefoot and draped in a shabby blue cotton frock and bonnet, she crouched to arrange a cloth on the ground and laid out her assorted wares. Once they were displayed to her satisfaction, she chatted to the prune girl for a while. Business was slow despite the crowds. Her only potential purchaser was a lady attired in a modest long black coat, hair tied up under a grey bonnet, a garb not out of place in church other than for her bright scarlet painted nails. She spent a time examining Lark's stock, said nothing and moved on.

Lark stepped onto her upturned barrow, rising above the throng.

"I am not here for money, but the good o' oor community," she shouted, getting immediate attention from a few passing customers. "My wares are less than a quarter the cost o' the shops. From my cart, a cargo o' the best value and finest quality goods in the whole o' Leith. Look at this magnificent length of the choicest French lace. Up the toon this will cost you five shillings a yard, but for you, madam"— she pointed at a stout, black-clad old lady who shuffled forward and inspected the cloth—"not even a shillin', not even eleven pence, not even ten, nine, eight, seven—aye , would you believe it—sixpence, missus! To you, a mere sixpence. Wear this and you are invited to the palace and not the poorhoose."

The old lady shook her head.

"I'll ask no more and I'll take no less."

The elderly lady turned away.

"What's a matter with you, missus? Have you got no money or have you got no brains?" Lark shook her head.

The woman dressed fit for church passed again. Now for the third time, Lark noted. On the fourth, she approached Lark's display, bent to study her wares again. Pins, bits of lace, knitting needles, a well-used man's shaving brush, cotton bobbins, garters, nutmeg graters, old shirt buttons.

The lady picked up a nutmeg grater. "This, how much?"

"Eh, fourpence," said Lark.

"Busy, are you?" said the woman.

"Naw, not really."

"Do you do this every day?"

"Naw, do other stuff as well."

"I'll take two."

The woman drew a half crown from her purse.

Concern on her face, Lark took the coin. "But I've not enough change, missus."

"You, my girl, have the loveliest green eyes."

Lark felt herself redden with embarrassment.

"Keep the change," said the lady.

"Oh, thanks, missus," said Lark, staring open-mouthed as the woman turned away and moved up the street.

Two hours later, the market over, Lark took a break before returning the barrow. She sat in a patch of pallid sun at the bottom of the Kirkgate. Bit into a nice red apple she had found discarded, content, with a whole half crown and a few coppers in her petticoat. Her family would eat well tonight.

When Lark considered it, other than where her next meal was coming from, there was only one subject on this earth a girl might fret about.

Men.

Was hard surviving in this world without stressing about them and their peculiar quirks. They were sometimes tough to read. She had observed the same with three brothers. Together, they were a bunch of tearaways, but William just moaned all the time. Wee Andy always had a smile on his face and never ceased talking. The third, Eck, quieter, invariably looked sad. Grown men were no different in their variety and moods.

Sometimes it was easy. Any girl knew in a place like Fat Archie's scrap shop, it was wise to be sure to have the wooden counter between you and him. Was obvious, you could sense it. Over the past year, others now gave her that look. Best avoid eye to eye, walk on.

Then others like her father before he died in his struggle with Mr Preston. When sober, he could be friendly even, sometimes had given her a hug. But when drunk, he was a violent monster, best given widest berth possible. The problem, of course, being that he was inebriated pretty well all the time.

Some men were scheming and dominating, like her big brother William. When not doing the odd day's work labouring at the wood yard, he would be out thieving or hovering around with his gang, making trouble. Then, at home, strutting about, telling everyone else how to behave, ordering her as if she were a servant and he head of the household with Father gone.

Alright, she knew being a McColligan offered protection, and it wouldn't be the first time William and his mob had battered anyone who gave her any problems, but it wasn't worth it. Her scorn for him had grown of late; she didn't want to be protected if by the likes of him. William and his crew just caused headaches for people. He needed taking down a peg. Always had been a bully, even when they were wee.

And as for that lumbering idiot Big Zander McFarlane hanging around with his blubbery lips and that irritating snigger. The audacity to make a pass at her a week ago. She'd told him in no uncertain terms to bugger off, but made no difference to that glint in his eye. She had even punched him, but doubted it helped. Lark's shoulders twitched with a shiver of dread, horror that he might push her into being shackled to someone with whom she had nothing in common and didn't want.

When she'd asked her maw, she'd just shrugged. "Men are men," was all she'd offered, then an afterthought: "Dinnae trust a good-looking man."

Good-looking men—a rare thing. Men only concerned themselves with their fighting prowess or how much drink they could consume. That bulging muscle did nothing for her.

Lark had thought about what she liked, decided she preferred the taller, lithe ones. That Charlie, the mud boy, was cute, had a friendly smile, though not very practical given relations between her family and the Prestons. Anyway, he stank of river mud.

Later that afternoon, she arrived back at Vinegar Close courtyard, which was, as usual, guarded by the two old women in their usual spot on the steps of Cherry Tree House.

"Give us a wee bit baccy for a poor auld woman," said Grannie O'Malley.

Lark lifted a pinch from the bag and handed it to the old lady.

"Is that all I'm getting?" she said, frowning.

"Aye," said Lark. "And consider yourself lucky, no much you get free in this world."

"Oh, my," said Grannie. "I'm sorry fer bothering you. I forgot I only exist when you need me for something like saving your wee sister with my herbs like I did last year."

Lark rolled her eyes. "You two are like the church bell with your whinging."

"Och, keep rolling your eyes. Maybe you'll find a brain back there," said Grannie.

"Aye, the trouble wi' you young yins is you never think aboot us auld yins," called a poker-faced Tin Pan Aggie. Then, once she mistakenly thought Lark was out of earshot, she muttered, "Aye, Miss Fuckin' Lardy Dardy wi' her airs and graces."

15. Flossie Tells a Story
Wednesday

Flossie McColligan

Lark stomped in and threw tuppence on the table. "Bloody rain last night washed all the baccy away."

"Not much to be done aboot that," said Flossie.

Lark shook her head. "Bloody tuppence. Unfair that we have to slog so hard for such a meagre living. Imagine if nobody was poor."

"Listen," said Flossie, turning. "That's the way the world works, so get used to it." She tied back her long auburn hair and gave the tiny fire a poke, blew on it. "At the top you have the wealthy, the shipyard owners, lords and bankers. Then its trades—bakers, shoemakers, shipwrights, carters and the rest, the members of corporations or societies. And then it's the likes of us—the scavengers."

A weary smile touched Flossie's lips. "And I suppose the poor sods working the workshops and mills or waiting each dawn for a job at the dock gates. After us, all the others: beggars, vagabonds or mud hunters like the Prestons. That's the way it is, how it's always been and always will be. We are lucky we are not in the poorhoose, and you're aware of life in the factories."

Lark shivered. In an automatic response, her hand drifted to the missing pinkie. She knew what factory work offered, saw it daily. Neighbours, others her age and younger, living as they did, eight to a room. Arriving home in a state of near collapse after a fourteen-hour shift. Saw it in their tired eyes, those dead faces. Also, injuries: fingers lost, burns, entire arms gone, and all for a pittance, little more than she made scavenging on the streets. No thanks, that's servitude. She'd tried it once. That was enough. A shiver passed through her, a memory of what happened that day to her wee friend Jean Armitage, an image she had blocked ever since.

"With your cigar ends and other bits and pieces, you may scrape a living, but at least you are your own boss—you like that."

"Aye, apart fae William's bullying."

Flossie drew together the oatmeal and added it to the pot of onions over the little fire she had made with their meagre supply of coal. Lark, Flossie and wee Eliza examined their limited supplies, the scarred vegetables and herring left over after the meal bought with yesterday's half crown—not much when split among six.

"Maybe William will bring food," said Flossie, hopeful.

Lark sighed. "Spoke to my big pal Beatrice. She said she could speak to Madam McPherson for me. She says it's good money."

"Aye, am sure it is, but get her to lift her skirts and show you her bruises."

Lark looked away.

"And soon she gets the pox or worse, then no use to anybody," said Flossie in a tone of peevish irritation. "No, times are tough, but we can manage. You stick to your tobacco along with what you make and sell until something better arrives. So dinnae even think it. We starve first."

It was cold and damp today after last night's torrential rainfall. The old stones of the dilapidated tenements in Vinegar Close radiated the chill, keeping people indoors. An icy squall whistled through, rain washing muck from the courtyard, leaving slippy remnants. Lark, her maw and wee Eliza spent the afternoon huddled around the fire in their spartan accommodation, all calm, William and the boys elsewhere.

Bare floorboards, a rickety bench and ancient padded chair with a table against dank walls, the bedding and sewing materials piled in the corner. Every room in the block had broken or cracked windows stuffed with rags or paper. Each room was rented to a different family: the new mob of Irish next door, the bootlace-selling woman and her five children above, the near destitute in the attic and across in Cherry Tree House.

"The fact is," Flossie said, "we are not badly off, with your cigar ends and trading stuff, William's labouring at the wood yard and thieving, and Wee Andy and Eck's rag and bone collecting. We make enough to get by. At least little Eliza here is getting fed, and it's been a blessing that, since your father got himself killed, he's not spending much of the scant amount we had on drink. I'm glad he's gone." She looked pensive for a moment. "Though I always understood why it turned oot the way it did."

Lark agreed with her mum, though it felt wrong to say it. Things were better with her father Abraham gone; they were not as hungry, and Flossie could sometimes afford a length of cotton to make their own clothes.

Lark hesitated. "Whit do you mean, it turned oot the way it did?"

Her mother appeared flustered for a second, brow crinkled, before exhaling a long sigh. She added a few tiny scraps of coal and a log of gnarled driftwood to the fire and dropped to the bench.

"I suppose you are auld enough to understand now."

Lark turned, eyes wide with curiosity.

"I think it's time you were telt the real reasons behind the Preston and McColligan's feud."

A silence as Flossie gathered the words.

"When I was young, my dad was a member of the Society of Carters. We lived in a respectable little hoose in Water Lane with my parents and sister. My father, a strict and severe man, the Bible his guide. My sister and I both nice-looking lassies. I remember the laddies always around us like bees to a honeypot, same as you." A wry smile crossed her lips. "Even Fat Archie McTavish, can you imagine, though wasn't quite so fat back then."

Lark grimaced at the revelation.

"But the yin I fell for was Earnest Preston, the younger brother of John Preston, who killed Abraham in their quarrel."

Flossie's generous mouth smiled at the memory of Earnest. "Such a Jack the lad, always talking, telling yarns, and with an infectious, loud laugh. Kind of a high cackle, but somehow sounded musical. A strapping laddie with lovely long blond hair, gorgeous eyes with a smile to die for. I thought us head over heels in love."

A frown crossed her brow. "But Earnest had no money and so my father wouldn't allow it. Said the Prestons would never be better than a bunch of mud scavengers. None of them good enough for his daughters. Then withoot warning, Earnest went to sea with no so much as a word. A few months later, a rumour telt he drowned in a shipwreck. Broke my heart. Confused and in a daze, I couldn't decide what to do, so I accepted Abraham McColligan when he asked me to marry him. My drunken husband. We married within forty-eight hours of him asking me. He appeared a decent man, even had a proper job with the harbour porters, but he lost that afterwards."

The light faded. A driftwood log rolled in the fire. Sparks of flame cast a flickering glow across Flossie's face in the gloom.

"Before I knew it, I was pregnant with William. Following his birth, to everyone's astonishment, Earnest Preston returned, and not only that, he was rich, had enough gold and jewels to set up for life. He only needed to glance at me once, and I found myself smitten again. But I had a husband and William now, so Earnest paid me little heed and took up with my younger sister, said he would marry her and pay my father for the privilege. For me, only jealousy and sadness, but with William to care for and with no option but to accept my lot, I kept away, never spoke to my sister and avoided Earnest."

Flossie turned her gaze back to Lark, who was listening with rapt interest.

"Then, after they had been together a short time, it ended. Yin morning I filled my carrier from the Water Lane pipe, with baby William on my back when I heard screams. Witnessed my father dragging my sister oot of the hoose into the gutter. The brute attacked her with a poker. She ran, blood on her face, him screaming and accusing her of being a harlot and a thief. I haven't seen her since that day. Was impossible to talk to my father when in a rage; he was also badmouthing Earnest, so I assumed he had run awa as well."

Flossie paused for a moment, rubbed her hands together with a humourless laugh.

"But Earnest appeared at my door the following day. Said he didn't understand why my father had attacked my sister. Said that all he did was to speak to her two days before and explained that their relationship was over and any marriage plans off. He had tried speaking to my dad to explain, but was refused entry to the hoose. He was at as much a loss aboot what happened between my sister and father as I."

Flossie paused and trimmed the fading candle.

"To my amazement, he then explained to me the reason he left her. Said he realised he still adored me and wanted to run awa with myself and William. I couldn't believe it. Overjoyed, sick with pleasure. I had never stopped loving him. Over the next few weeks, we met in secret and planned for oor escape; he came to the hoose when Abraham was working at the docks. Told me of his riches, said that on his travels he saved an auld gypsy's life and in payment received a treasure map. Found where it lay buried and dug up gold rings and bracelets along with a huge, beautiful jewel. With William a baby and Abraham having started drinking, I was confused, uncertain what was best. All I knew was I still loved Earnest and that he now said he loved me."

A note of anger in her voice, though she was quick to suppress it.

"Abraham discovered Earnest and I had met, so we had a blazing row. To make matters worse, my father was incandescent with rage when he found oot I'd been seeing Earnest again. Father, a man of few words, but he came to my hoose. Among his confused rambling, he said he would kill Earnest, and refused to talk to me again, saying I had made my bed and that I should sleep in it."

Flossie's expression hardened further. "Earnest and I decided we were going to run awa with William. He bought tickets for the London boat, then a day before we were due to sail, Earnest is arrested and thrown into the auld Leith Tollbooth."

"Whit had he done that's so terrible?" Lark's eyes were wide with interest.

Flossie's face became grave. "Someone told the authorities that Earnest's money wasn't from buried treasure but was from the rewards of piracy. He had sold a gold ring to fund our new life. The magistrates said they had linked the ring to a king's merchant ship attacked and robbed off the Barbary Coast a year past, passengers and crew murdered. They searched his lodgings and found his gold, linked it to a reign of terror carried out by the pirates. Though yin jewel was never recovered, apparently the most valuable of all.

"I assumed my father must have learned the truth about the piracy and turned him in. But afterwards, a rumour spread that it was my husband, Abraham McColligan, wha was to blame, and that's when it all started. The Prestons were raging, and so the feud began. It's never been the same since between the McColligans and the Prestons.

"But Abraham always denied that he was behind it, though I'll never ken who betrayed Earnest, whether it was my father, husband or else someone different altogether. They both had a motive to cause Earnest harm. From that point, Abraham was at war with the Prestons and turned more and more to the drink. My dad refused to speak to me again and died a short time later, while my sister never returned."

Flossie wiped the tear forming in her eye.

"I was lost. Pregnant with you by then. Then, over the following years, Eck, Andy and Eliza were born. Abraham held onto his harbour porter job for a while, but he worsened, always in a drunken stupor. After Earnest had gone, I hoped Abraham and I might have worked it oot and start again. We lived in the same hoose but were never together. Abraham's drinking got worse, and I just felt a gap in my life. Though no choices, given my situation. I believed it hadn't been Abraham wha betrayed Earnest. Eventually, he lost his position at the harbour along with everything else and we ended up here. The last years, it became worse and worse. He started seeing things, he even talked of visits fae Earnest's ghost, though I dinnae ken if that was guilt that he had informed on him or else his mind becoming addled with the drink."

"Earnest's ghost?" said Lark, bright eyes alive with interest. "Whitever happened to him?"

Flossie took a deep breath to steady herself, shook her head.

"He was cast in chains wi' a bunch of other pirates on Leith Sands. They left them there until the tide rose and the waves drowned him. I couldn't face it and went nowhere near. My father, Abraham and Archie McTavish were in the crowd, but I've never asked them aboot it. I didnae want to ken. Before it all happened, Archie, Earnest and Abraham were firm friends."

"Maw, do you think you will ever marry again?"

Flossie mused for a minute. "Doubt it, whit's being gained? Unless to a nice, rich man."

"I see the way men look at you, reckon you can still turn a head."

Flossie smiled and then a silence, only broken by the mutterings of Eliza as she played around the fireplace.

"I'd like to get married one day, but cannae imagine to wha," said Lark.

"I think oor William has got someone in mind for you."

"Big Zander." Lark grimaced. "You're joking, though he's started taking liberties, seems to think we are already a couple, although I've telt him several times we are no. Hasn't got it in his thick skull. I even hit him but he just grinned that stupid grin."

"You have plenty time for that. Best not worry, just make sure that whoever you choose doesn't drink."

The pair pulled out a narrow roll of cotton and threaded their needles. Annie's blouse had fallen apart, and they now cut out the good parts to patch Wee Andy's shirt. Any remains would be used for floor and dish cloths. From the cotton roll, Flossie fashioned a shape for a new slip for Lark.

"And there's another thing concerning Earnest I want to tell y—"

A sudden rumbling and thump of heavy boots outside, and William stumbled through the door, his beefy frame filling the space, his face like an angry bull. He stabbed his finger at Lark.

"I heard Charlie Preston was trying to talk to you after the floating church." He scowled.

"Nothing was said."

"If that ever happens, I'll beat you black and blue as well as him. Dinnae you dare. He's a Preston and you're a McColligan, you remember that."

Flossie stepped between them and met his eyes, voice cold. "Get off her back, William."

"Dinnae you tell me whit to do," he snapped. "Now dad has gone, you will throw it to any man wha fancies it."

Lark shot forward and slapped him hard across the jaw.

"Dinnae you dare speak to Maw that way." Rage turned her face beetroot.

William stepped backward and raised his fists.

Lark stomped out.

William breathed deep and lowered them again. He gave a scoffing laugh. "Fucking wimmen."

He turned to his mother. "Whit's for eating."

16. The Superintendent Takes Action
Thursday

Superintendent Andrew Angus

Superintendent Angus remained standing to attention, his eyes on the wall above the fireplace.

"I can assure you the shipowners are not happy," said the Police Commissioner, sitting legs crossed at the other side of the room. He threw a cigar end into the roaring fire before lifting his wide rump from the seat. The expression on his decrepit, creased features as dark as his fine tailored suit.

Mr Adam White's broad beam swung as he prowled the room, a film of sweat glistening on a retreating hairline above sagging jowls.

"You need to see the bigger picture, Superintendent Angus," said White, tone light. "My aim when I become Provost of the newly independent town of Leith is that it prospers. The shipping company's senior director has visited me here in the Town Hall more than once and has laid out the implications with absolute clarity, explained in greatest detail."

He stopped in front of the superintendent.

"The ship is one hundred and twenty feet long. A beautiful wooden paddle steamer with the very latest advanced side-lever beam engine. Appears it has a steam pressure of fifteen pounds per square inch, is schooner rigged and carvel built and offers the remarkable top speed of ten miles per hour even in a headwind."

White's voice hardened. "The senior director was also at pains to explain that the main source of company profits nowadays is the provision of comfort for first-class passengers. Nice linen and crockery, stunning rooms with soft beds and lounges, sofas upon which they can relax. All in a colour co-ordinated interior offset with handsome brass fittings and gorgeous dark mahogany framework and trimmings."

The volume rose further as the commissioner circled Angus. "Plans were afoot to fit out the upper deck staterooms of the handsome new ship in that finest mahogany. And now the entire project to be set back months, months I say."

White was now shouting. "And why? Because the Leith police can't stop the constant thefts from the docks."

Angus could feel the spray of spittle on his ear, along with a whiff of the commissioner's hair oil.

"And do you know who it's really, really, really an unwise idea to get on the wrong side of?" Now stood directly behind him, Angus's superior screamed at the top of his voice, "The Leith and London Steam Packet Company!"

Then a silence, only the ticking clock and flicker of the fire. Mr White moved to stand again in front of Angus, dark eyes boring into him.

Then, a knock at the door, and a bespectacled clerk popped his head into the room. "There's a Mr Black to see you, Mr White," he said, before quickly closing it again.

Did Angus detect the commissioner looking for a moment flustered before quickly composing himself?

"So, get out of my sight and do something about it!" shouted White, his nose almost touching Angus's.

The superintendent saluted and turned to march out the room.

***

After hours of enquiries, the only information Angus had gleaned made little sense. His single witness was a night watchman at the yard on the north side who reported a barge containing extended lengths of timber moving during the night. That had to be it. And despite the distance, the watchman was adamant he had seen only two men aboard. But how could two men have loaded that timber so quickly? It just wasn't possible. Must have involved a whole squad. Then where did they come from? As if he didn't have enough worry with the recent murders.

By early evening, still daylight as the shadows lengthened, Superintendent Angus had the full complement of eight constables at the ready. They assembled by the old drawbridge at the end of Tollbooth Wynd. Equipment was checked and instructions given before swiftly moving along the quay.

With the harbour packed, the Shore was alive with sailors and girls without hats, many of the "jolly tars" drunk and spilling out of the quayside public houses despite the early hour. Angus had to step over three lying flat-out in the gutter. Then, up into Queen Street and right to Bowie's Lane and their target: the lodging house frequented by the casual dock labourers, itinerant traders, passing sailors and other human detritus. From the narrow lane into the narrower vennel, through the labyrinth of squalid ancient buildings known as Old Babylon, home to the lowest of the low. A place to where fugitives from justice were drawn like a magnet.

A group of labourers smoking short pipes. One spat chewed tobacco at Angus's feet. The crooked lane hung with dangling dirty white clothes above where unwashed, shoeless children played leapfrog. Barrow boys with carts leant against the wall and two young lassies with scabs on their legs sat underneath. A painted girl swore as they passed a colourful group on the steps of Madam Flora's place at the entrance to the lane.

"Oooh, it's the fucking boys in blue," a tubby one laughed. "Look out, girls—it's the mutton shunters arrived to try to shunt some mutton." She lifted her skirts provocatively to peals of laughter from the others. Angus and his squad ignored them and pressed on to the far end of the passage.

The sign hung on two short chains from a pole above the peeling narrow entrance. "The Swan Hotel", better known as Mrs Archdeacon's Dosshouse. Eighty lice-infested bunks crammed to the rafters in the back rooms.

Superintendent Angus was first through the door. "Police, nobody move!" he yelled, truncheon drawn.

The first room was a large kitchen. Clothes hung from the ceiling: a wet shirt and a torn pair of once white trousers, grubby brown with tar. The accommodation was so full of smoke that the ray of evening sun from a skylight resembled a lance cutting through fog. A hearth of brick now pure black, like the beams spanning the ceiling, and a floor of packed earth with bench seats occupied by a dozen dozing men.

Two boys knelt by the fire toasting mackerel. The whole place stank of it. Another sat struggling to dry out a cigar end.

A big man with matted grey hair and a double chin stood up, grimy and unshaven, dressed in an old woollen smock. "Whatever it wis, it wisny me," he blurted.

A sly-looking bearded one in a once plush red waistcoat fidgeted in his seat. "Didn't saw nuffink."

Angus grabbed the skinny boy with the cigar and pulled him to his feet, hand a firm grip round his throat.

"A late-night job loading timber. Two nights ago, tell me who."

The youth trembled. "W… w… was a timber merchant, said it's a rush job and paid us each a florin."

"Oh," said Angus with sarcasm. "A job, in the middle of the night? And you didn't notice the watchman of Ramage's yard lying in a crumpled heap, knocked out cold? Did you not think that suspicious?"

The boy was shaking. The others looked at their feet.

For the next forty-five minutes, each of the lodgers was sat on a chair, smacked about the skull and questioned (in that order). An hour later, as the bell of St Ninian's struck six, Angus and his squad stomped back onto the Shore, Angus's expression grim, exasperated that he now had little more than he knew already. The only useful information was that one of the pair was heavy and did the talking, the other skinny and said nothing. Both wore masked hoods throughout the entire operation.

It had happened again. Angus kicked a fish box in frustration. They were always a step ahead. Worse still, his supply of snitches was dwindling. What he hadn't shared with his constables or reported to his superiors was that he hadn't only lost the lawyer discovered in the drain at the Stinking Pig. The previous two dead bodies were also his informers, all, it appeared, poisoned by the same method.

A pattern was forming, whenever he received information. By the time he acted, it was always too late, the crime already committed. There must be a mole in the police ranks somewhere, an individual on the inside telling them his moves in advance. But where and who? That Archie McTavish was involved somehow. He was working for someone else. Angus was sure of it, but how could he prove it?

17. Archie Impresses a Potential Employer, and We Meet Arabella and the Mysterious Mr Black
Friday

Arabella Deveraux

That evening, Fat Archie McTavish had another important job. A task undertaken on behalf of the organisation he hoped would soon become his new employer, should he successfully complete his apprenticeship.

Friday night was rent night. Often time-consuming to get the books to tally as certain individuals were less keen to part with their hard-earned cash than others, but then how long is a piece of string?

To the Kirkgate and the market first. The small-scale black marketeers paid their dues without challenge, never any problems, the traders aware that refusal would bring swift justice from the Fraternity. Any stupid enough to cross them would be discovered up an alley, with shattered bones or, for the less fortunate ones, a dagger in their back.

Many established businesses had also concluded it prudent to furnish themselves with the extra security the Fraternity offered, given the significant level of lawlessness in the port. The incompetent police seemed powerless to curb it, but if Fraternity customers ever had problems, men appeared with masks and clubs and the problem resolved itself. Providing this security had developed into a growing side of company business.

Archie visited most shops in the street, happy at his work. Liked to gossip with the storekeepers and shopgirls. Everything was going to plan. A bright future possible, Flossie McColligan and him ensconced in a little cottage somewhere away from the river stink. *You may like the life you're living*, thought Archie, *but it's nicer to live the life you like.*

The light faded. Shopkeepers in leather aprons started to raise their shutters, so Archie moved onto the brothels. First to Madam Flora's house in Old Babylon. One of the lesser establishments. Meagre and dreary with sparse furnishings above a dingy tavern patronised by the lower classes. He passed a queue of drunken sailors, stevedores and soldiers, then nodded to the thug on the door with cudgel in hand. Inside, clustered around a table, were half a dozen tired-looking pale young women with pinched faces. A pair supped on tea, potatoes and fried fish; another slumped half asleep. Girls half-robed, cheeks hung with melancholy, though with no appearance of shame. Seldom allowed out, these thin young woman in skimpy dresses were given little money. Often drugged and made to sign some papers before being scantily clothed, on occasion fed, and worked hard in the stable-like rows of grubby stalls in the rooms above.

Archie pocketed the cash from the surly, unsmiling madam, a ghastly-looking plump harridan, better dressed than her girls, with a crumpled, over-powdered face.

"We can't charge high rates in this place," she griped. "Your fees are too steep."

"The prices are not my department," said Archie. "I'll send my superiors to confer with you."

Madam Flora turned away with a sigh of resignation.

"You need to try harder," said Archie. "And remember, big things have wee beginnings."

Next, onto a much more respectable house, very discreet and tucked up a vennel off Burgess Lane. A tall labyrinth of a building with several entrances that offered its gentlemen visitors a high degree of discretion when attending appointments.

Here, Archie liked to linger. He enjoyed the company, the large kitchen a homely scene with a warm fire in the grate and an air of cleanliness, order and comfort. The wall with hooks, on which hung an assortment of gowns, petticoats and bonnets, and from the adjoining parlour, the sound of a piano playing Mendelssohn's latest.

Two pleasant-looking young women sat at the table, chins leaning on their hands, looking curious and smirking, while another cut her nails with a knife. On the table were candles. One girl was at the fire with her gown over her knees, displaying a cream underskirt. A rope hung over the fireplace, hung with stockings, blouses and undergarments. At the table, one of the young women wore a blue jacket, with striped kirtle and crinoline. The other resembled a genteel shop girl with a cotton frock and apron, teapot in hand.

Archie offered his most gracious smile. "Ladies."

The girls burst into a titter they struggled to suppress.

Archie was aware that while these women usually lacked education, they had ability. These young ladies were expensive and, if lucky, could make a reasonable living. For them, the job was a means to an end. They often sought marriage once retired.

Madam McPherson ushered Archie into the next room, furnished with handsome chairs, thick curtains and sofas. Over-perfumed and respectable, Madam McPherson clucked like a mother hen, fussing around him. Archie was apologetic as he accepted the coins.

"Don't worry about little old me, Archie. Remember, when the Lord closes a door, somewhere he opens a window."

However, at the top of this building there lived a lady who Archie was aware didn't pay. She offered very specialised services. Archie had only glimpsed her once. He dreamed that if he played his cards right, he may one day rise high enough in the organisation to join that select group who might enjoy her favours.

***

Arabella Devereux's flat was on the top floor of Madam McPherson's establishment, filling the roof space. Fine accommodation with views to the river, quality curtains and chandeliers, the best furniture: wood and polished brass grand enough to belong in a palace. With the prices she charged, she needed very few gentlemen callers these days, only a privileged few with speciality tastes. She had funds aplenty hidden away, and now her work was more about duty to her employer than any kind of necessity.

Her employer? A man she had once loved, had always respected, was now dependent on and, although she knew him so well, still feared slightly. He would arrive soon.

While she waited, she thought about the men in her life. Her employer hadn't been her first love—that was a young lad from her home town, a distant memory now. But in a way, her employer had saved her, offered a new life after that darkest of episodes. She had known many nameless men since she first met him (and had clear memories of the dead ones), but she'd never found another true love like him. Working for him now, in this way, she could still stay close.

Her beautiful light-blue silk dress rustled when she moved across to the bed and opened the bedside drawer, revealing two boxes. She lifted the smaller, with its red mother-of-pearl dragon design. She raised the lid. Graceful fingers with scarlet painted nails lifted the contents. It sparkled. The fingers caressed its smooth surface, felt it take on the warmth of her hand, tested its weight. Arabella would be sorry seeing it go after so long.

A knock on the door. The company she had anticipated entered. A reticent gentleman she had known for many years; they had been sweethearts in Paris in her younger days. An infrequent visitor to Leith. Members of the Fraternity knew him as "Mr Black".

Arabella was always surprised by how plain he looked, sharp features but a forgettable face, like a clerk in a bank or the post office. Apart from his eyes. That was what had attracted her from the beginning. Dark grey but so sharp, spirited, intense and alive.

Arabella was one of the few people to know his real name, though, despite their many years together, she had never shared with him that her own name was actually Jeanie. Not that anybody would recognise her now from when she last answered to that moniker.

As always, he was clad in black. Quiet-spoken with a deep, low accent she had invariably found appealing. Solidly built, with a slight limp Arabella knew was from a wound he had received at sea when in the Far East. He'd made his fortune running opium into China for the East India Company.

Many myths about Mr Black had developed over the intervening years. A man who sparked curiosity in others, with a talent for ambiguity. One rumour claimed he became a priest, another that he had been a fearsome pirate and leader of the most vicious band of cutthroats on the high seas. Another that he owned a hidden island inlet on the West African coast, selling captives as slaves. Another, he was a devil worshipper. There was even a tale that he was the bastard son of Marie Antoinette.

Of course, Arabella was aware that while there was a grain of truth in some of these stories, they were largely either false or else gross exaggerations his fraternity had encouraged to develop a sense of mystery and fear among any criminal competitors.

Arabella smiled and whispered his real name as she leant forward and pecked his cheek.

"So how is business?"

"Almost complete," said Black. "Our company has achieved what we set out to do here." He smiled an admiring smile. "And in no small way thanks to your efforts."

Arabella blushed, embarrassed by the praise.

Mr Black and his colleagues had, over time, learned to live by a simple philosophy that he had always thereafter adhered to. Make money. Then, through unrestricted trade in various commodities, create more wealth. More money meant more power. Money and power, could you ever have enough?

Mr Black came from humble beginnings. His father was a barber from Marseilles, one of the handful of Protestant Huguenots remaining in France after the massacres of 150 years before. For this reason, a prowess in secrecy became an ingrained family tradition—a skill put to further use when taking advantage of the complexities following the defeat of Napoleon Bonaparte in 1815, before making substantial gains from the power vacuums that followed the struggles between various revolutionary, royalist and church powers. Gains that over time contributed to Mr Black taking a prominent role in an international and secret organisation now dominated by the Huguenot diaspora stretched throughout Europe.

Mr Black and Arabella had rekindled their friendship a few years before when Arabella moved from Paris to Marseilles, where Mr Black now held court. He was now the only gentleman caller who didn't benefit from her usual services, but a man who fully appreciated her talents. Who liked to make use of her other capabilities. It was in his interests to ensure she was kept happy and able to operate with impunity, safe and without fear of interference.

Their meeting today was brief. He gave her a name. "Only one task this month, a man of the cloth this time."

He took a small packet from his pocket. "And for you." He pressed it into her palm. "In payment for your loyalty, and success with the lawyer in Riddle's Close. For the best, only the very best." He offered a thin smile. "Soon your work here will be complete."

Arabella took the package, held it to her breast. She gave him a light kiss on the lips before he left.

She returned to the bedside drawer and added the packet to the larger box with a green leaf mother-of-pearl design. A special treat for later.

***

The clock tower in the distance chimed midnight. Archie McTavish replaced the three floorboards in the corner and pulled the bale of horsehair on top. Tonight's rental takings had been added to the Fraternity's strongbox he kept tucked under the floor.

He'd lifted his keys to close up when a late visitor tapped the window. Archie suppressed his surprise when he saw who it was. A rare honour indeed. The visitor was dressed in black and limping, a large peaked cap casting a shadow over his face. When removed, it revealed a face initially unimpressive but soon confident of its power, lean and with sparkling eyes that appeared dark blue, but when the light caught them, you saw they were actually grey. A man who lived in the shade, and a rare visitor in Leith. Among the local criminal fraternity, his name was only ever mentioned in hushed tones and never within earshot of anyone outside their inner circle.

The only source of light was a blackened oil lamp, the visitor's features dim in the shadow, the flame catching his piercing eyes. Archie looked at the floor, thinking it wise not to get a good look at his face. Many of his future colleagues already established in the Fraternity had never met him; a few didn't believe he even existed.

"Lock the door," said Mr Black's deep voice. "We don't want to be disturbed."

Archie obliged.

Black sat in Archie's chair and fixed him with a steely stare. "Back when you were a boy, the thirteen ancient corporations of Leith— the Shoemakers, Hammermen, Fleshers and the rest—would decide when men worked at their trade, where they should work, the wages paid and the prices charged."

Archie nodded.

"Those days are gone, Archie. The Mariners, Carters and the other archaic trade societies are unsuited to the modern world. The future belongs to the adventurous. Investors, industrialists, producers, they are what's required, and will bring great wealth for some. The secret? Join the adventurers."

Mr Black pulled a cigar from his breast pocket and lit up. "However, there is still a place for ancient codes of honour, as is the case in the only fraternity that continues to prosper in this new world, the fraternity you are soon to join. Tomorrow, in fact."

Archie felt his spirit lift, wanted to break into a smile. He glanced at Black's face and decided against it.

"You have done well in your apprenticeship, Archie, so the good news is we will recruit you as a foot soldier. The name of our organisation, you will soon learn. You know that our tentacles now spread into every nook and cranny in this port and beyond. Smuggling, robbery, protection, illegal gaming, prostitution or any other vice you can think of. And through these activities, we provide a freedom that enables everyone to trade as freely as they wish and so succeed in life."

"I… I won't disappoint you," stuttered Archie, struggling to contain his joy.

"And we keep the wheels of the economy turning. You see, Archie, it's all about growing the pie. If we make it as big as is possible then we all gain. Obviously, our organisation takes a small percentage." A thin smile creased Black's sharp features. "But the wealth trickles down, so everybody benefits."

Archie experienced a rising excitement that he was soon to take the oath; the chest hidden under his floorboards would overflow with gold rather than silver and copper.

"But first you must understand our organisation, Archie. We members of the Fraternity are merely a company of free traders whose influence happens to have spread over time. Our simple technique being to bring order and control to all criminality in key port towns, a business model we have found to be an efficient way to ensure unrestricted free trade in its many forms. It greatly improves the flow of goods, and aids in the removal of restrictive trade practices by those who want to block that trade with their tariffs, taxes or laws. Profitable supply chains can be developed for every commodity, including those others may think undesirable. A local version of our secretive structure is replicated wherever we operate in the world, and that now includes the port of Leith."

Black sat back, lifted his head and blew a cigar smoke ring to the ceiling. "The strong survive, Archie. Our business model ensures our organisation's powers and profits grow, and leads to many other benefits. Now, influential men can be bought as necessary, already powerful men offered financial backing at a price, good men can be corrupted, weak governments brought down if required."

He lifted his head and his eyes bored into Archie's. "Though crucially, Archie, a key priority is to keep the organisation's profile so low that it remains invisible. That is important, Archie. We have recruited you because of your local contacts and local knowledge, but we wouldn't have if we didn't think you could keep your mouth shut."

For the next few minutes, Mr Black provided new instructions. A supply chain to be expanded in future. Potentially very lucrative, a small-scale project at present now ripe for further development.

Mr Black stood to leave, then turned and put his hand on Archie's shoulder.

"Remember, Archie, it's an oath that is never broken." He lowered his voice to a whisper before slipping out the door. "The Oath of the Fraternity—of Unholy Blood."

18. Archie Makes a Promise
Saturday

Archie McTavish

Earlier that day, there had been an expanse of blue sky before clouds rolled in. Now the light had faded, and it was gloomy and dark in the cramped, crooked lane. A weak glow came from a few windows above; a wet rain battered down. Archie kept to the shadows, face concealed, wide-brimmed hat tugged low. He found the door and knocked three times as instructed. It opened with a creak, and a grey faced man beckoned.

He was grabbed from behind, a bag tied over his head. Without a word, they pulled him along a corridor, dragged him downstairs, then more stairs, the atmosphere cloying, musty and damp. The sound of hushed voices, and he was hauled through a doorway.

The blindfold was removed. Archie covered his eyes, dazzled. The light from a carpet of candles spread across the walls and a large table with a small silver cup in its centre, surrounded by hooded men in black cloaks.

"Repeat these words," said a deep voice behind him. "I, Archibald McTavish, swear by my blood to honour the Fraternity."

Archie stuttered as he repeated the phrase. Someone grabbed him by the hair and forced his head to the table. Other hands pulled his cloak, tore his shirt, baring his arm. He felt a knife slash, gritted his teeth.

"I will be loyal to the Fraternity. Never interfere with other's interests. Never inform."

"I swear," squeaked Archie, and he repeated the words.

The blade bit his skin again

"Be rational. Don't engage in battles you can't win."

"I swear."

"Be a man of honour. Respect Fraternity elders."

He felt the knife bite a third time. Had to stifle a cry, then echoed the words.

"Keep your eyes and ears open and your mouth shut. Show courage and heart in the face of all adversity."

After repeating, Archie pulled back up. On the table, the silver vessel was half filled with his blood.

"With this blood, I do swear," said the voice. A prod from behind.

With a trembling hand, Archie picked up the cup.

"With this blood, I swear the oath, the oath of the Unholy Blood."

Archie repeated the words and drank with one gulp. The taste, metallic and sweet.

The voice behind, now louder. "To break the oath is to die."

The hooded figures repeated the phrase in unison. The blindfold returned. They dragged him back out the room into the corridor, a puff of rancid breath on his cheek.

"Was a famous philosopher," said the voice, "who said that nothing taught by force stays in the soul. But that doesn't apply to you Archie McTavish. You now have no soul; it belongs to us."

With that, they yanked him back up the flights of stairs. He heard the entrance being opened, felt a rush of fresh air, the rain beating, as he was pushed into the lane. He drew off the blindfold and held it to his bloodstained upper arm.

"Never return here," said the grey-faced man who'd admitted him. "Instructions will follow."

The door slammed in his face.

Archie let out a long sigh. His arm stung like crazy. A smile formed on his wide lips.

"I'm in," he whispered aloud.

His mind shifted to future rewards, and thoughts of that nice little cottage and a new life—with Flossie McColligan.

19. Angus's Lucky Find
Sunday

Superintendent Andrew Angus

It was dark and wet, a sharp squall funnelling down the river from the west, a biting wind.

"Enough," said Angus. "Nobody will be out in this weather."

He held up the storm lantern, lighting the sagging face of old Constable Ross, shoulders drooped, soaked and deflated, sheltering in the lee of a stack of timber.

"Let's head home."

They left the jetty and headed for the dock gatehouse, their footsteps echoing on wet cobbles. A sudden, unexpected sound carried by a gust of wind, the tinkle of breaking glass coming from the warehouses. They turned to the industrial yards and caught a whiff of tea and tobacco when they stepped between the big sheds.

Angus stopped to listen again. He pointed and whispered, "Constable Ross, I believe it's this one. You go around the other side, keep your wits about you."

Superintendent Angus crept forward, ears straining for any sound beneath the noise of wind and rain. He could sense it. Careful and quiet, he drew out his truncheon. He turned down his lamp and kept to the darkest shadow.

A creak above. In the gloom, the top window opened. He pressed himself flat against the warehouse wall. A leg emerged, then another, followed by a whole body, which pulled itself out and dropped in front of him. Angus stepped forward and lashed out with his baton, heard the crack of teeth. The figure slumped against the wall. He swung again. The shape went down.

Angus was quick to run his hands through the pockets. In the second, he found a wad of banknotes, and slipped them into his own pocket.

Another creak from above. Angus stepped back into the shadow, every nerve alert. A second shape clambered out the window and dropped to the ground. A vicious punch to the face, then a cudgel pressed to the throat, forcing him back. Angus held up the lantern. A young lad, gasping, face red. Angus put down the torch, rummaged his hands through the youth's pockets. Nothing.

The lad could only gag, powerless to reply. "Who's been a naughty boy?" whispered Angus.

The truncheon pressed hard against the boy's neck. Angus considered for a moment, released his grip and stepped back. The boy gasped for air. Angus took a kick at him, half connecting as the lad scrambled away, legs pumping as he darted between the warehouses.

Then Constable Ross's heavy footsteps.

"Constable Ross, come quick. There were two of them. I've nabbed this one." Angus pointed at the prone figure. "But the other devil escaped. Quick—search him, check what he's got."

The constable rummaged through the grounded youth's clothes. "Nothing, sir."

Angus stuffed the wad of notes deeper into his pocket. "I'll be dammed. If they have stolen anything, it must be the one who ran has it. Better call out the watchman. He can open up and see what might be missing."

They cuffed the first young man, pulled him groaning to his feet and dragged him towards the dock gates.

Later, back at the Town Hall, Angus filed his report. Forty five pounds stolen from a coal merchant's office on the docks. One criminal apprehended but unfortunately the other slipped away with the loot. Superintendent Angus had another thought, stopped. A bead of sweat formed on his brow. Then he smiled a thin smile before heading home.

20. Charlie Intervenes
Monday

Charlie Preston

Light had faded, and Charlie splashed to the ladder on the quayside wall. He'd stayed on when the others had gone home. Took much cajoling, but after an hour of effort he'd pulled the rusted hoist hook out from right under the paddle of a Leith Hamburg and Rotterdam Shipping Company steamer. Just in time, before the tide rose too high. He could feel the weight in it—a nice chunk of iron it was, too.

He thought of Lark, caressed his chin, the spot where she'd touched him last week. He considered the unique colour of those emerald eyes, her cheekbones' graceful curve, those ankles, that thick red-gold hair.

The Shore was deserted after the afternoon's heavy rain. It had cleared the air, leaving only the river stink. Dark now, but for the rays from the gas light outside the New Ship Inn that sent a glow across the cobbles. Charlie thought about popping in the sailors' ale room— it sounded busy with drunken calls and heavy-booted dancing—but decided against it. At the top of the ladder, he swung the hook onto his shoulder and stepped out for home.

A muffled scream further up the roadway in the gloom, some sort of altercation. Coarse laughs and shouts, people up ahead moving and calling out.

"Get off, you bastards!" a female voice pierced the air.

Charlie recognised it. A clang as he dropped the hook and set off full pelt along the Shore.

Two drunk sailors—Germans? No, more that London twang. The big one had Lark off her feet with his arms around her waist.

"Alright, me little honey?"

"How much do you charge?" said the sly-looking skinny one swaying in front of her, a wide grin on his florid red face.

"Fuck off!" screamed Lark.

"Right," said the big one, tattooed with a bull neck and a scarred bald head. "Enough negotiating. We've tried asking nicely."

Lark kicked out and caught the sly one on the side of the head.

"Ouch." He laughed. "Well, she's a wild one. Get her up the alley."

Charlie ran at full pace, naked feet skimming over the cobbles. For a moment, the flash of realisation—fighting was never his forte—then the thought was gone. He accelerated. In the gloom, they didn't see him coming until he arrived. Charlie charged into the big bald one holding her, connecting with a flying headbutt. Blood spurted from the sailor's burst nose, and he and Lark staggered backwards and sprawled on the road.

The skinny seaman took a wild swing, so drunk he swayed and missed. Momentum sent him tripping over an old fish box and landing with a thud on the quay.

Charlie pulled Lark to her feet by the hand. "Run."

Face like chalk, Lark was frozen to the spot.

The sly sailor was back up. He lunged forward. Charlie weaved to his left; the man grabbing thin air. Charlie pushed with both hands. His assailant fell backwards, collapsing on top of the bald one, on his knees as he tried to rise. Charlie followed up with a kick to the bridge of his already bloody nose. A loud crack.

"Run!" cried Charlie, and shoved Lark away.

She took to her heels.

The skinny one, up again, staggered forward, shaking his head, confused. Charlie ducked below his swing and tripped him. He toppled and crashed onto his knees, skull thumping against the wall.

The piercing sound of a police whistle echoed around the buildings. Charlie danced from the melee of fallen, drunk, shouting sailors, cutting up the narrow vennel and working his way through the tangle of alleyways away from the Shore. Breathing hard and shaking, he found a nook beside a midden and waited until the commotion died down.

Much later, he returned for his iron hook. It lay where he'd dropped it.

21. Lark Remembers
Tuesday

Lark McColligan

New dawn, thought Lark, *a new day.*

The room was cramped. She'd already emptied the piss pot and rolled her blankets and hung them up on the wooden pegs before nibbling on yesterday's crust. A hint of river sewage mixed with the whale stink from the soapworks as she took in the view through the cracked window. Lines of billowing laundry stretched across the courtyard, a bustle of workers shuffling to jobs in docks or factories. Others with long leather water carriers over their shoulders, toing and froing from the standpipe round the corner in Brickwork Close. Voices of people shouting, babies crying or family arguments through a window left open.

Lark often perched here on her favourite stool. Passing boys would glance across and try to catch her eye. They never did, she with more entertaining things to observe. Sometimes old Grannie O'Malley getting out of bed, surrounded by her dried herbs, or leaning out her window puffing on the first pipe of the day, the ground outside like a midden strewn with boxes, broken bottles and muck. Or the huge Irish clan over in the front room of Cherry Tree House drinking and arguing, or the new Highlander family above them with their praying.

Lark enjoyed people-watching from a distance, whether she was seeing what they had for breakfast, the colour of their underwear or with whom they'd had a discreet liaison. If she later met these neighbours in the street, it amused her. They wouldn't know how much she knew of them.

The sun broke through, so she moved outside. Time to roam. Would be more careful following yesterday's scare.

"Oooh, so how's Miss La De Da today?" said Tin Pan Aggie.

"A wee bag of tobacco," said Grannie O'Malley. "Is that all you have from yesterday's scavenging? A lassie like you should be oot doing proper work."

"Aye, so you should," said Aggie. "And I'm telt that you young folk are getting well fed at that Floating Chapple. Well, whit aboot us auld yins?"

"It's only for the youngsters," said Lark

Grannie shuffled, scratched the large boil on her nose, stroked her wispy beard, hacked, then spat. "Aye, well, we are children as well, the children o' God."

Tin Pan Aggie's face wrinkled as she threw Lark a fierce scowl. "Aye, it's ridiculous what you young folk get up to nowadays, with your flouncing aboot the yard. It's not so much fun when you're auld like us, so you remember that when you get to oor age."

Lark giggled. "So, I should do a proper job, just like you pair sitting here every day?"

"Well," said Grannie, insulted, "you weren't saying that when those herbs I spent hours searching for helped your wee sister cure her bad lungs."

"How many times are you going to mention that? I've paid you times over with the tobacco I've given you these past months."

Grannie pulled out her pipe. "Aye, well, give me a fill from that wee bag you've got."

"Anyway," said Aggie as Lark handed Grannie a pinch, "we are too auld. Work's a youngster's game. You should get employed in a factory. I heard there're jobs going in the glassworks and the ropery—and your poor mother with these laddies to bring up and look after. Nae wonder your family is always starving and in rags."

"Tried that and got this," said Lark, holding up the four-fingered hand with its missing pinkie. "So, no thanks." She gently stroked where the finger had been. "At least we have a room to live in. You stay in a coal shed at the back of Cherry Tree Hoose."

"Well, do you think I dinnae ken that? Would you listen to Miss La De Fucking Da," said Aggie with a grunt. "It's alright for some folk."

Lark turned. "I did factory work, at the ropery last year."

She wished she hadn't said it. The vision blocked from her mind now flooded back.

"How long for?" said Grannie.

"Half a day." Lark clenched her teeth, face reddening.

Aggie and Grannie glanced at each other, confused. Tears pricked Lark's eyes.

"Do you remember wee Mary Armitage who used to live at the top of Kemp's Lane? I worked there with her, and I'll not be doing it again."

Grannie O'Malley drew on her pipe. "Why is that? Too much like hard toil, was it?"

Lark's face fell, and she peered at the ground. "We were in this enormous room filled with noisy machines. I was on the winches. Crushed my pinkie. Mary came across to help when her apron caught on a spinning shaft. It dashed her to the floor."

"Och, well, she should have been more careful," said Aggie.

Lark raised her eyes. "Then it whirled her round and round, the crack of bones snapping above the noise." She stopped, took a slow breath, fighting her emotions.

"She was crushed."

Tears welled in her eyes.

"Pah," said Aggie.

"Her body pulled tighter and tighter within its works, blood scattered over the frame."

The vision filled her mind. Poor wee Mary's body dashed to pieces and mangled, the shape jammed between the machine and the floor. Lark felt sick.

"Harrumph," said Aggie. "Well, maybe she might have tried the mills rather than the ropery."

"So, why don't you work in a factory?" snapped Lark. "Am never working in these places again, would starve first, and if I went back, there's no baccy—so think yourself lucky."

Tin Pan Aggie gave a huffy shrug as Lark threw a fierce glare before turning and stomping out of the courtyard.

"Huh, proper work's too good for the McColligans," said Grannie. She hacked, struck a lucifer and spat before relighting her pipe.

"They are too busy oot thieving, I'll bet. Or that mother o' hers will be in their hoose sitting by a big fire, aye, heating her rent book while we're oot here in the freezing cold."

"Harrumph," said Aggie. "Miss La De Fucking Da, right enough."

The first drops of the threatened rain pelted down, and the two old women shuffled under cover.

22. Meetings and Muggings
Wednesday

Charlie Preston

Charlie had already visited Archie's scrap to sell old iron. A high tide along with recent heavy rain had left the river a murky brown torrent, so no chance of mudding today. A thin sun broke through. Charlie passed the scrum of porters and row of carts lined up to take a big shipment of wine unloaded from the decrepit smack at the wharf. No market on Wednesdays, so he sauntered towards the docks to see what was to be found.

Outside the gates of McKenzie's Yard, Charlie watched a gull make a pass to the end of the pier before it ascended to an updraft and curved back in his direction. Then, he literally bumped into her. Astonished, he stumbled over a broken creel, almost knocking Lark over, but caught her by the wrist to stop the fall. Instead of giving him a mouthful, she grinned.

"Thanks for whit you did on the Shore on Monday. Think you showed up just in time."

Charlie blushed. Lark turned and walked on, eyes down, scanning the ground. Charlie followed, the obvious thing to do. He skipped along beside her. They wandered in silence. Charlie was surprised how relaxed he felt, initial nerves gone. It seemed natural somehow.

"We Prestons have been doing mudding for generations," he said. "It's amazing, the interesting things to be found. It requires a good touch, ya ken; you cannae see much, so have to move your feet and wriggle your toes along slow until they detect something. Sometimes even a tiny wee thing like a nail—tricky if feet are freezing."

Lark stopped to ponder a moment. "Mmm, hadn't considered that. Street scavenging is more paying close attention. It's surprising whit people leave lying around. Look at this." She whipped off her bonnet. "Found this last week, beside the midden next to the Stinking Pig. Got a good label, hardly worn."

Charlie examined it, impressed.

"It's about learning the patterns," said Lark. "People follow a routine in where they meet and whit they leave behind. Whit do you do when the tide is in? I've seen you at the market some days."

"We Prestons do anything. My big brother Tommy borrows a cart and I sometimes help finding something to fill it with and sell. Maw's too auld for the mud now and works up at the dust yard, so I help her, too."

"When I'm not doing cigar hunting, I do selling as well," said Lark. "Barrow boys let me work for them flogging stuff. Last week rabbit skins, the time before umbrellas, clay pipes and garters, the week before glass and old crockery. If there's nothing else, I do lucifers or sometimes Fat Archie has given something on tick, though the crook takes nine pence in every shillin' you make, so it's no worth it."

"Aye, same here," said Charlie. "Reckon I've sold almost everything there is to sell; it's just whatever's going. Apart from the mud, I like doing crossing sweeping the best, ootside the hotels or theatre, clearing a path through horse dung so rich folk can cross the street. But then, last week I was helping my big brother sell auld knives and forks and shirt buttons. The time before that, it was rat poison. This week, Tommy's got tea trays and herring toasters. The other good one I wouldn't mind trying is flogging pretend smuggled goods. My big brother Tommy is great at it—profitable if you can pull it off."

"How does he do it?"

"He dresses up with a peaked sailor's hat and kerchief round his neck along with a hooped shirt. He gets the cheapest handkerchiefs but pretends they are top quality silk that's been smuggled. It's amazing how many folk fall for it; they walk away thinking they have a bargain but have actually been robbed. He puts on the disguise, and Tommy has great patter. He sidles up beside an unsuspecting customer and says…" Charlie mimicked his brother. "Hey shipmate, I've just returned from a long voyage, so splice me and shiver me topsails. I smuggled these all the way from Bombay. You can have them cheap before I'm nabbed by the custom hoose pirates wha are after me. Well, helm a lee, let's turn into these shallows and I'll show you a bargain."

Lark's pretty lips giggled.

"He takes them down an alley and gives them a story about him rushing to leave toon on the next tide so the sale has to be in secret and done quick so the customer doesn't see whit he's buying. The mug's convinced he is making a great purchase until he gets them home. It's incredible how many folks are taken in. Folk love to believe they are getting a bargain."

Lark laughed out loud. Charlie thought it the sweetest sound he had ever heard.

They stopped. Lark waited for half a dozen apprentice boys outside the New Ship Inn to finish and discard their cigar ends. She stepped in once they had moved off.

"I've also done a bit horse holding and usually the fields at harvest," said Charlie. "I might get a proper job one day, wouldn't mind doing lamplighting if the chance comes along."

"I've done other things as well," said Lark. "Me and my wee brothers tried the tannery for a while, twelve hours stretch plucking and scraping the hides and doon hauling water. Though I prefer easier stuff, pasting up posters or street mending. My wee brother Eck and I did it for a bit—anything, fixing broken china, or tea caddies. Or sometimes me and my maw make things to sell. Maw's good with her hands, she teaches me. We produce fly papers in the summer, or children's doll house furniture, women's caps. One day, maybe I'll be rich and I could find a nicer place to live."

"What aboot your brothers?"

"Och, they are alright. Apart from William—he's always throwing his weight around. Does a day or two labouring in the wood yard, but it's all aboot nicking with him. Now Maw's worried he's leading on Wee Andy and Eck and they will copy him. I haven't telt her half the stuff I ken they get up to."

"Aye, tell me aboot it," said Charlie. He fingered the fading bruise on his chin.

"Though his thieving has fed us at times, but she's concerned he's getting entangled with real bad yins."

"Have you ever tried a factory?" said Charlie. "Never done it myself. I enjoy being oot in the open air."

"I worked the ropeworks once, but I got this." She held up her four-fingered hand. "Was my first day, became trapped in a winding machine. My wee pal was killed in an accident. I won't be going back. I've heard the mills are worse. I'd rather starve. Wha kens, one day might get a proper paid job, but no' a mill or factory when you see whit it does to folk. I reckon I ken at least a dozen people missing fingers or even an arm."

"Ouch," said Charlie. "Ach, you dinnae need it. In fact you look better withoot it."

Did she just blush?

"And whit's with you and Big Zander?" said Charlie, concern in his eyes. Lark shook her head and looked at the ground. Charlie decided not to push further, unsure if that reaction had been a positive sign or not.

They found a sheltered spot among a big consignment of wool stacked near the end of the pier and sat for a while. A smart three-masted barque was leaving. Wind rattled its rigging, only a jib to the fore as it slipped out the harbour mouth. Then the sound of halliards being run through blocks as its huge sails rose, a crack of canvas as the ship lurched onwards. Timbers groaned as it cleared the piers, surf pounding the bow and the following gulls losing interest. A hoot came from a paddle steamer that slowed to let the barque pass.

"Wonder where they are going," said Lark

"No idea," said Charlie. "Could be London, maybe Dunbar, or India."

Charlie inched a little closer on the bale of wool.

"I'd like to go somewhere," said Lark. "But dinnae have a clue where anywhere is, and I can never leave my maw. She needs me."

"Mine too. I don't know how they manage what they do. Mine's better off withoot oor auld man."

"Same here," said Lark. "I never liked him, anyway."

"Aye, in a way, I'm glad it ended how it did, though could have been less messy."

They sat in silence looking over the harbour mouth, the constant movement, craft large and small coming and going.

"Only a few days till the Floating Chapple," said Charlie. "That meat last week was the best." He salivated at the memory.

Lark twisted and met his eyes, expression serious. "Though there's something odd with Reverend Ponsonby, way he looks at you."

"How does he look at you? He seems to mostly dance around when he's preaching."

"Mmmm, dinnae ken, it's just funny. And that wee lassie Annie Green who vanished a few weeks ago."

"What aboot her?"

"I noticed him staring at her at the Chapple. Strange, couldn't take his eyes off her."

Charlie considered for a moment and shrugged.

By the end of the afternoon, Charlie was enjoying himself, with an awareness that the only thing he wanted in future was to spend more time with Lark McColligan. He had helped her gather a respectable sack of tobacco and escorted her towards home. They strolled up the Kirkgate and turned into Brickwork Close, stopped at the water pipe.

"Can I meet you tomorrow?" said Charlie.

"Why not? So long as William doesn't catch you."

"I'm no scared of him."

"I am, sometimes. Best avoid him spotting you."

"How about the same place we met today? And Lark?"

"What?"

"Can I kiss you?"

Lark blushed and put her finger to her lips. "Mmm... well... maybe. Just this once."

So, he did, and that was a fine end to a splendid afternoon. He knew without doubt it was something he craved to do again.

***

For a moment, Mr Preston, the banker, appeared doubtful. He stifled the expression before opening his mouth.

"But you can't eradicate poverty. It's just not possible."

Both in heavy overcoats against the chill, Dr Thomas Latta and Mr Alexander Preston stood on the south bank at Coal Hill, observing the dark, stinking river. Today, it was a torrent after the past day's deluge of rain and high tide. Choppy black swirls and eddies tore towards the sea. The cables holding an ancient cargo boat and sleek trader strained against the force of the debris-filled froth that squeezed between the quay and hulls. The air was heavy with the stench as the pair leant over the wharf edge to examine the filthy, churning mass below. This close, their eyes watered.

Dr Latta, serious brow dark, hesitant, a tension in his chiselled jaw. Standing so close made him dizzy. He'd always feared turbulent water since near drowning as an adolescent. But today it might be worth it. He hoped this meeting could be a new beginning for his project.

"You see, Mr Preston, the river is adding to the suffering amongst the poor. The problem is that the factories and mills further up discharge all kinds of foul matter. The dyeworks, distilleries, quarries, paper mills, printworks, together with the sewage produced by the inhabitants of

Edinburgh. What you end up with is a substance of the most odious and abominable character, that sends acrid and fetid emanations into the atmosphere—smell it."

Mr Preston sniffed, a shiver on his double chin. "Yes, agreed. It's pretty foul, but it has been worse. With the stink from the breweries and blubber boiling, there are days we kept the doors and windows of the bank shut."

Dr Latta's dark brow turned and faced him. "You see, my colleagues and I, our studies have indicated that the mortality in the streets bordering the river, as compared with those away from its banks, is much increased. Those in the immediate neighbourhood have a significantly higher rate than those living a short distance away. In fact, our investigations have established that the death rate among children under five years who live close to the water's edge averages around one in seven, while those who reside in the same class of streets a short distance way is one in twelve."

"A sobering figure," agreed Preston. "But explain, sir, how does this concern the bank?"

"Our study has shown that the Water of Leith contains ten times the quantity of organic matter found in the River Thames at London Bridge. The gases and vapours from our estuary are potential killers."

Preston took a step back. "That's possibly correct, but you can't halt the march of progress. The factories and mills create our wealth, so are vital, and therefore it's imperative they get the power required from the river. So, why would we want to stop them?"

"I used to fish here as a boy, now not a fish to be seen," said Latta. He turned and looked Preston hard in the eye. "What I require is an investment. There are premises in Quality Street where I plan to open a hospital, one available to all, including the poor."

They stood for a time longer, mesmerised by the torrent. Dr Latta thought Mr Preston may have lapsed into an offended silence.

"A hospital for the poor," said Preston with a glance of bemusement. "Then you need to make appeals to a charity or philanthropists to fund such an enterprise. I could approach members of the Kirk Session and ask if anyone has suggestions."

"What I am looking for is investment, not charity. A healthy workforce is an efficient workforce."

Alexander Preston's squat frame sagged, confusion on his brow. He took off his bowler hat and cast his hand through thinning hair before replacing it.

"Even if true, how can your scheme make money? So, it is not something that interests the bank. We are concerned with the march of progress," said Preston. "What would my colleagues' view be if I thought otherwise?"

"Please understand, it would be progress. And it's not what other people think that determines who you are."

"Well, if you arrange an appointment at our Bernard Street office next week and bring me your figures, we can discuss it further."

A grimace touched Dr Latta's narrow lips. "It's not only the river; there's cholera on the way. You could say, given today's conditions, it's the perfect storm."

"Cholera."

"Yes. It's travelled from Russia, and on to Hamburg, and now Sunderland. It's merely a matter of time before it reaches here. We have taken precautions, but it might be here already. It could ravage the town."

Preston lifted the chain and glanced at his gold watch. "Grim news indeed. However, I must be off. Much to do."

"I'll accompany you part of the way."

The two men turned away from the river's edge. Ten eyes watched from the end of the wynd.

"Two toffs coming our way," said Deek.

"Could be a bad news day for some folk," said William, an unfriendly grin crossing the wide features under his battered stovepipe hat.

"Right, lads," he said, turning. "Get in position, the usual routine."

***

After the kiss in Brickwork Close, Charlie was walking on air. He wanted to do that again, didn't want today to end. So, he followed her into the labyrinth of lanes and wynds.

"You should go," she said. "If William finds you on his patch, you know what he is like."

"You're right, but can I have another ki—"

"Hey, mud boy! Where are you going?" shouted a scrawny urchin who stepped in front of them.

Charlie looked around. He had been so absorbed with Lark he hadn't realised he was now halfway along Vinegar Close—in the heart of McColligan turf.

"Get lost!" screeched Lark. "Leave him alone."

"There's a mud boy in our close," cried the lad.

"You better go," said Lark. "He will call William."

A shout behind. Charlie turned and saw two much bigger lads from the McColligans' crew.

"Hey, it's a Mudder!"

The scrawny boy tried to block him. Charlie shoved with both hands, sending him sprawling. Another of their big lads came stumbling from a narrow vennel further up,

"What's he doing here? Get him!"

Charlie turned—and ran. Long limbs pumping, he tore to the end of the close into Giles Street, the thump of the gang's footsteps on the cobbles behind. The road ahead was closed off by a horse and cart loading outside the soapworks—no alternative but a sharp right into Cables Wynd. Charlie galloped round the corner into Sheephead Wynd, and a sudden skidding halt. The route was blocked, a tubby little toff on the ground, Big Zander McFarlane sitting on his head, Deek holding his legs and Eck McColligan raking through his cloak.

A tall, younger toff had Wee Andy clinging onto his back. William roared, "Bring him doon," tailcoat flailing as he swung his cudgel. The toff blocked with his cane.

Charlie glanced behind at the three big lads bearing down on him. Only one way to go. He charged into the fracas. A flying kick sent William, the younger toff and Wee Andy sprawling, a tangled crash-landing together in the gutter channel in the centre of the wynd. Wee Andy's face smashed against the gutter's raised edge, blood and teeth bursting from his mouth, mingling with thick, congealed sewage. Charlie, up in a flash, thrust his heel into William's face as he tried to rise and forced him careering backward. Charlie seized the toff's hand and pulled him to his feet.

Still armed with his cane, the toff thrust forward and swung across Eck's face as he rummaged through the tubby man on the floor's cloak. He gave a squeal as the metal tip slashed his cheek.

Charlie lunged and kicked Big Zander full on the chest. With a gasp, he rolled off the little fellow's head, leaving him floundering. Charlie swung at Deek before he and the tall toff backed off two steps as the three youths in pursuit joined the fray.

The neighbours above were now peering out their windows, drawn by the commotion.

"Shout for the mutton shunters," cried the old man on the top floor.

"These bloody laddies," screeched a skinny wifey on the other side of the lane. "Aye, I can see them—ah ken wha they are. Where are the polis when you need them?"

With their backs to the wall and outnumbered, Dr Latta and Charlie took up a defensive posture. Latta raised his cane; Charlie, jaw clenched, lifted his fists. The McColligan crew were seven flushed faces, screaming threats, throbbing veins in their necks, Wee Andy McColligan still on the ground groaning, teeth shattered. William at their head eyed Charlie with a tight-lipped grimace. He rubbed his chin and flinched.

"You, Preston," William growled.

Charlie bared his teeth, said nothing, fixed him a steely glare. He could sense William calculating, weighing up the odds. Then, the shrill note of a whistle, a blur of blue coming out of Fox Lane. William and his troop picked up their bloodied wounded, turned and ran.

Dr Latta skipped forward and pulled Mr Preston to his feet, a cut on his head and in a daze, his handsome coat mud-streaked. Breathing heavy, Latta turned to Charlie.

"Our praises, young man. I dread to think what would have resulted if you hadn't appeared."

Charlie glanced at the approaching uniforms. He spun and set off at full pelt towards the river.

"If I can ever repay you—" shouted Dr Latta after him as he disappeared out the end of the lane.

Mr Preston was unstable on his feet. Superintendent Angus, surprisingly swift with his bandy gait, arrived, drew out his notebook. Coming up well behind was old Constable Ross, panting.

"Anything missing?" said Angus.

Preston, his face pinched, checked his pockets. "Not much. I've still got my wallet, so only a few florins. Oh, and a rather nice silk handkerchief, had my initials embroidered and was a gift from the bank. So, no real harm done."

"Little bastards," said the superintendent. "As if I didn't have enough on my plate."

He considered a moment.

"Do you think you might recognise them if you met them again?" He peered at Preston, the banker trembling and blowing hard.

"I believe so. Got a good look at the leader in the stovepipe hat, would know him if I saw him again."

23. The Superintendent and Arabella Find Answers
Thursday

Superintendent Andrew Angus

Superintendent Angus, wearing his best frock overcoat to mask the police tunic beneath from prying eyes, tugged his hat over his brow. He stepped with care, the recent heavy rain leaving the crooked lane muddy, and rubbed his palms together, anticipating what to come. Muscles twitched with excitement. His windfall meant regular visits to this place in future, rather than the rare occasional treat.

A glance up the empty wynd, aged bricks towering into the blackness above. Pitch dark but for the single lantern above the discreet entrance. His hand was cold on the brass as he tugged the bellpull and waited. A black cat passed. Its steps made no sound, the light reflecting on bright yellow eyes as it scurried away. Another sideways glance checking the coast was clear, and he yanked the bell a second time. The unsmiling, crumpled face of Madam McPherson answered with a creak.

"Oh, it's you." She beckoned him in and pointed up the stairs.

Angus blew on his hands, glad to be in the warmth, took a sharp breath and set off up the narrow spiral staircase to the garret room on the top floor. He stopped outside the door, barely able to contain his excitement.

There was something about her, he had decided. The dusky looks and exotic French accent, the quality of her clothes. It calmed him. He sometimes felt he had known her for years. He knocked and entered.

Arabella Devereaux sat back in the chaise longue, dressed in the finest yellow silk gown. Her luxurious dark hair tied in the latest French style, rosebud lips, aquiline nose, fine long fingers tipped with scarlet-painted nails. A thin smile greeted him. The room was furnished with comfortable chairs, a sofa, handsome patterned drapes and glass chandeliers.

"Arabella," said Angus, a sheepish grin on his thick jaw.

Arabella sat back and observed, face impassive. She raised her eyebrows. Angus sniffed, and ran his hands through his hair, stiff with oil. With a wheeze, he straightened his coat, doing his best to look dignified for the serious discussion he had planned.

"Arabella, I need to come right out and say it. I have feelings for you," he said, his eyes pleading.

Arabella stifled a laugh.

"Please, Arabella, I'm serious. I suggest we have an arrangement, a regular agreement, where I can call on you at short notice when the need arises."

"Superintendent," said Arabella. "Remove your coat and sit on that chair."

Angus tugged off the heavy frock coat and hung it on the hook on the back of the door. Arabella sat forward on the chaise longue opposite him, lifted her skirts and revealed her knees. Angus licked his lips and broke out in a sweat.

"Now, Andrew, I told you when I chose to admit you to my favour that I'm happy to have you as one of my occasional gentlemen callers. And you likewise know that it will delight me to perpetuate our infidelity with impunity, but also, I'm sure you agree it would be unwise for it ever to be unmasked. I would hate for your professional reputation to be compromised or tarnished."

Angus's shoulders slumped. "B…but can't we…"

"If you wish, it is possible to make our arrangement a little more exclusive. Now, if you agree to buy me a modest house overlooking the park and pay me four thousand guineas a year, you can visit anytime, and we might enjoy regular outings for dinner or up to Edinburgh for the opera."

"But, Arabella…"

"Did I ever tell you that my father was a stern and heartless man?"

Angus shook his head.

"I have had little education other than the Bible and stick, but as you know I have certain 'talents'. As well as those of which you are aware, I also play piano and have a decent natural singing voice. However, when I was young, I made a choice. I might have trained as a seamstress, or worked in a shop, but my weakness was I liked dresses and fashionable bonnets."

Angus took out a handkerchief and wiped perspiration from his face.

"My parents were stupid and uninterested in me, so one day, after I had some personal difficulties, I made a point of leaving my home town and moving to Paris. There I met a young businessman of influence. That gentleman made me an offer, which I decided I couldn't refuse. The rest, as you say, is history. For years, France was my home, until I was invited to come here. Over time I met Madam McPherson, who you saw downstairs, and we have now developed an arrangement that suits us both."

She nodded at the small bowl on the table. Angus took out his pocketbook, pulled out two one-pound notes and placed them in the dish. Arabella stood. Her hand went to the clasp at her neck. The dress dropped to the floor, revealing her naked, pink-skinned, healthy-shaped body.

Angus gasped. The candles flickered. Sweat formed on his brow.

"Oh, there's been a rise in price," said Arabella. "It's now two guineas, seven shillings and sixpence."

Angus fumbled in his pockets for the additional coins. Arabella took his money and placed it in the drawer by her bed next to the two mother-of-pearl boxes where she kept her most precious possessions.

Arabella spoke, voice firm. "Now get your trousers down and yourself bent over that couch with your arse in the air."

She strode forward and reached for the heaviest of her collection of riding crops. Then came a loud crack as she swung hard.

"Oowww," said Superintendent Andrew Angus, tears of joy in his eyes.

"And afterwards, you can lie on the bed and I'll rub ointment on your bottom. That relaxes you, removes your stresses. Then, tell me all your troubles at work; I find it a fascinating subject and I'm happy to hear every detail. I've always found that a trouble shared is a trouble lessened."

24. Archie's Visitors
Friday

Archie McTavish

Fat Archie was asleep at the shop counter, the fire warm. A door banged, and he woke with a start, almost fell out his chair. It was not the visitor he expected.

William swaggered in with a pair of that gang of young tearaways he hung around with, his sturdy frame dressed in a decent-looking old-fashioned tailcoat and topped with a battered stovepipe hat. His two sidekicks, the lumbering Big Zander and skinny, scrawny Deek, had ragged, dirty grey shirts and that scruffy feral look. Archie had warned William once before.

Archie stood, stepped to the door and popped his head out for a quick glance up and down the muddy lane. The air was nippy; the rain had worsened as the day wore on—never got light—and now the afternoon gloom engulfed the little row of shops on Broad Wynd. Still busy, though, with people coming and going from the baker's further up, swathed in heavy winter cloaks, a few wealthier ladies with damp, drooping bonnets. A group of laughing, drunken sailors stumbled past, ignoring the destitute huddled in doorways, caps in hand. Archie shut the door.

"Alright, Archie," said William with his cocky, lopsided grin.

Archie said nothing. Big Zander McFarlane picked up a worn bottle from the rows on the shelf and gawked at the label. Archie took two steps forward and, with a solid headbutt, sent him sprawling. Zander's nose burst open. He fell over a pile of coiled rope. William and Deek stepped back, stunned.

"You stay," Archie said, pointing at William.

Archie stamped a heavy boot hard on Deek's bare foot. "And you, go, and take him with you." He nodded at Zander, now floundering, fist clutching a broken nose.

Deek stifled a squeal and staggered backwards, pulled Zander from the floor, and hobbled outside as fast as his bloody foot allowed.

"Now, William," said Archie. "You're a fine lad; you and I can enjoy a constructive working relationship. However, if you're telt to only ever come here alone, whit I mean is that you only ever show up on your own." He moved forward until his great bulk had William cornered. His hooded brows darkened as he stared deep, William trembling with sudden discomfort. "Our line of business is never to be carried oot in public." He bared his cracked teeth. "Do you understand?"

William nodded.

"What you must learn, William my boy, is nothing is free in this world. Someone always has to pay, whether it's with the finest courtesan or with the cheapest whore on a bed of straw on a stable floor. The times they are changing. The days of the ancient societies, the Carters, Shoemakers, Fleshers and Mariners, have ended. Nowadays it's not aboot trades and corporations, it's aboot discovery and adventure. A land of opportunity for a laddie with your abilities, and no requirement to run awa to sea in this case. All you need is capital."

"And you," he said, stabbing William in the chest with an unfriendly finger. "You now work for my fraternity, the yin operated by myself and my colleagues." He moved his face closer, offering a whiff of rancid breath on William's cheek. "And some day, if you play your cards right, you may even become a member, if you can get it into your thick skull"—he gave William a firm rap on his head with his knuckles—"that oor organisation only ever operates in secret."

Archie pivoted and returned to his seat behind the counter. He warmed his hands at the fire. "So, whit have you got?"

William pulled a necklace, a jewelled ring and a handsome silk handkerchief from under his shirt and laid them on the counter. Archie lifted his eyeglass to inspect the jewellery.

"Very nice," he said in a whisper.

The silk handkerchief was of the best quality; he recognised the embroidered coat of arms of the Leith Bank alongside the letters AP.

"Oooh, a nice silk hanky and adorned with initials—and see that insignia! You have been aiming high, my lad."

Archie took coins from the box under the counter and placed them in front of William, then stood and patted him on the back with a friendly smile. "Now, tomorrow's job is arranged. You ken what you need to do, and then I'll see you at nine o'clock next Thursday in the Stinking Pig's basement. Mr Roberts, the landlord, will let you in if you tell him you're seeing me. By then I've likely another job for you related to oor new scheme."

William lifted the silver and scurried out the door.

Archie had concluded that William would soon outlive his usefulness. He might arrange for the Fraternity to use the McColligan boys up in Edinburgh somewhere; there's always a demand for pliable thugs. Then, once the girl was gone, it would just be Flossie and him. He'd search out a little home by the coast, sitting with Flossie in a tidy garden, roses around their front door.

Archie's next visitor was old Grannie O'Malley. She shuffled in, glanced up, moved to the hearth and spat. She took a small bottle from her sleeve and placed it on Archie's desk.

"Dwale," she said.

"The auld ways are often the best," said Archie, picking up the bottle and slipping it into his pocket.

"Gall bile, hemlock, wild neep, lettuce, opium and henbane." Grannie grinned through her pair of teeth. "A dose o' that will put anyone to sleep."

She held out her hand. Archie dropped in the coins, and she shuffled out.

Archie's third visitor was the one he had been expecting. Was hard to recognise at first, with a flat hat pulled over his eyes and a nondescript black cloak.

"You would think you preferred to avoid being recognised," said Archie, his tone patronising.

The young Reverend Ponsonby's eyes flashed angrily for a moment, then he smiled a nervous smile. He rummaged in his cloak and placed the gold sovereign on the counter (the one that he had discreetly slipped out of the poor box at South Leith that morning). Archie picked it up and bit.

"The same arrangement as usual?"

The reverend nodded. Fidgeted. Archie could sense his discomfort.

Archie didn't reflect on his motives. A strange little man, though a regular paying customer, treated as any other.

What Archie wasn't aware of was that Ponsonby's evident nervousness didn't relate to any lack of trust in their business arrangement. More his sense of rising excitement at the notion of tomorrow night. An opportunity to participate in an activity he'd found was the sole way to satisfy a yearning that ate away at him. Despite many prayers, he had never found an answer as to why, or where, this longing originated. Only an awareness that it was the only method he'd ever discovered of not feeling totally alone.

"I arranged your choice for tomorrow night," said Archie. "She is one of eleven. The father drowned at sea last year, while the mother's heading for the poorhoose, doubtless won't even notice she's gone."

The reverend nodded and turned to leave. The door burst open and Superintendent Angus barged in.

"Oh, oh..." stuttered Ponsonby, sounding fearful. He turned away and clutched the counter top. "Eh... mmm... eh, what a fine-looking handkerchief. Oh look, it's even got my initials. Can I purchase that, my good man?"

"Just going to check your backyard, McTavish," said the superintendent. "Another big consignment of sugar gone missing last night."

Angus opened the yard gate and moved out of sight for a few seconds before returning.

Archie shook his head and raised his eyes to the ceiling. "You will find nothing on me," he said with a scowl. "I'm sure the good reverend here can vouch for my impeccable reputation."

"Evening, Reverend," said Angus, nodding.

Ponsonby smiled a weak smile. The superintendent frowned at Archie but said nothing more before striding out the door. Ponsonby let out a breath of relief.

"Oh, and Reverend?" said Archie.

Ponsonby turned back towards Archie.

"I telt you previously, but I'm not sure if you understood."

Ponsonby looked confused.

"After you have finished having your fun, I've got to sell them on to my colleagues up in the toon."

The reverend shook his head, still not understanding.

"You overstepped the mark last time—so don't damage the merchandise too much."

The reverend's eyes widened. "I... eh... I..."

Archie grabbed him by the lapels and pushed him against the wall, stuffed the embroidered handkerchief into his breast pocket. Archie bared his yellow teeth with a smile that was as welcoming as that of a hungry wolf.

"Or I might have to damage you."

25. Lark's Challenge
Saturday

William McColligan

A piercing hoot came from the little steamer as it left the jetty, churning waves in its wake.

"Neeps! Neeps! Farthing a neep," cried a brawny young lad with a basket, and a lustier shout—"Fresh, penny the lot!"—came from a fishwife with a child on her bosom, holding out bags of oysters. A youthful girl standing on a stool called, "Apples, fine apples! Apples a ha'penny."

A pair of naval officers with braided epaulettes and boys carrying heaps of cakes on trays jostled with uncultivated sailors with their smokes and ale outside the Britannia tavern, lecherously eyeing a couple of shabby women they could have for a shilling.

Saturday was payday, and the monthly market was doing a roaring trade in a watery sun. Stalls of combs, brushes, toys, jewellery and iron tools, all crammed together the length of the Shore. Halfway down was a busy clothing stall manned by a pair of dark-eyed Hebrew boys, with racks of well-used greatcoats, gamekeepers' coats, frock coats, green velveteen dress coats, and deep blue pilot coats. Behind them, button hole menders and cuff shorteners sat on stools, stooped over their tasks with needles in hands.

All social classes thronged the Shore. Gents in top hats mixed with groups of ragged, unwashed urchins in tattered oversized coats and greasy black caps competing with the gulls, pigeons and stray dogs for anything discarded. Vendors swarmed among the crowd with vegetables and eggs, casks of vinegar, sacks of carrots and spices, tables with screws and nails, and piles of worn shoes amid heaps of old clothes. The crowds and bustle were overwhelming.

Some costermongers had become men of substance with carts and horses of their own, squeezing through the crowd to bring in more supplies for the shops and stalls—heaps of onions, tatties and cabbage. The smell from the flesher's stall—pigs' trotters, blood and offal—mixed with the river stink.

Saturday also a busy day for William and his crew, now proficient in any style of thievery. Working as a team, they dressed for the occasion, William in his usual blue tailcoat and stovepipe hat; Zander wearing a grey frock coat, scruffy tweed trousers and a peaked cap and shoes; Deek, Wee Andy and Eck McColligan barefoot but in clean, short jackets.

Wee Andy was studying a jewelled broach on old Mrs Lafferty's stall.

"Bugger off," she said, tugging a shawl tight around her, being well aware he had no intention of purchasing. Wee Andy looked up and smiled. "Bugger off if you're not buying, ya wee toe rag."

Andy picked up another pendant. The old woman reached across the stall with her hand raised. "Look, you little bas…"

Deek, waiting in the wings behind, nipped in to snatch a ring and bracelet while she was distracted, and Andy vanished into the crowd.

Next was a toff, a gent with generous whiskers. The five of them closed in, a wolf pack. They eyed the tail of the gentleman's coat. Too easy. Sometimes they would go for watches in waistcoat pockets if it was crowded enough. William hung back as the 'looker' in case of any police, Andy and Eck on either side. While Deek stepped in front of the man to distract and cover, Eck slipped in his hand and lifted his pocketbook. Before he had time to react, the wallet was passed to Big Zander, heading the opposite direction, William positioned to block if any pursuit. On this occasion, the gent just stood, bewilderment on his lavish eyebrows, aware something had happened but not knowing what.

In the afternoon, the boys returned to the Vinegar Close courtyard loaded with sweets and cakes with which to impress and share with William's growing group of female admirers. Any jewellery or watches they'd later take to cash in at Fat Archie's.

Being a Saturday, the yard off Vinegar Close was more crowded. A few labourers with an afternoon off. William and the boys were fooling around the courtyard, being annoying, but Tin Pan Aggie and Grannie O'Malley had said nothing as they sat in their usual spot on Cherry Tree House steps.

Then it started, innocently enough. Wee Andy had given William cheek as he was lighting the half cigar he had slipped from Lark's bag that morning.

He struck and raised the lucifer. "Slap him for that, Zander."

Wee Andy tried to run, but Zander lunged and grabbed him by the scruff of the neck and lifted him off the ground by his shirt. As Zander drew back his hand, Lark sprang out the stair door with her quick, graceful tread.

"Stop!"

Zander stopped; William frowned.

"Slap him, I said."

Zander's brow creased, confused.

Lark stepped forward and, in one fluid movement, snatched the cigar from William's mouth and turned to Zander.

"Let him go."

Zander looked worried, then blushed.

"Slap him, I said!"

"Don't slap him."

Zander gave Wee Andy a slap that was more of a pat on the cheek and released him. Lark kept her eyes on William, a frown on her face. That might have been a sneer, but she said nothing.

Wee Andy scurried away. William's brow furrowed and he raised his chin, a twisted smile on his lips. Lark stood her ground, staring him down. There was silence, then, with only the smallest movement, Zander made a half step in her direction.

William's eyes widened.

"Four fingered bitch," he growled.

Lark laughed her infectious laugh, then turned away with a dismissive wave of her hand. She strode out of the courtyard and headed for the Shore, looking pleased with herself.

William's eyes swung to Zander. Zander looked at the ground and spat.

"'Ave got to go. Need to help my maw lift stuff at the dust yard," he mumbled before turning away.

Well, thought William as he stared after Lark, his eyes dark. *That has finally decided that.*

"Hmmm," said Grannie O'Malley.

"Miss La De Da better watch oot," whispered Tin Pan Aggie.

Grannie hacked, pulled out her pipe, then spat.

26. Charlie Makes a Move
Sunday

Charlie Preston

Charlie woke among the breath of others. It was still dark. He slithered out from among his brothers, tiptoed over his wee sister and mother and out into the lane. Warmer today, the overnight rain had stopped, but the wynd was still muddy. He sat on a quayside bollard at the Shore as the bell of St Ninian's chimed six. Being the Sabbath, the river was deserted before dawn, other than one lonely boatman in the gloom, oars silently rising and falling.

Charlie's thoughts battled each other. Deep down he knew that if his love was sincere, he needed to be honest and ask her to her face. Did what had occurred between them mean anything, or was Big Zander McFarlane her choice? Or was that just what William wanted?

He sat an hour thinking, arguments for and against, moods changing as he considered options and how matters might work out, stomach churning at some. The first glimmers of sun hit the river, and he made his decision. A great deal of thought was given to what he was to say. He imagined himself telling her how much he had missed her smile, and that she being a McColligan and him a Preston wouldn't matter, despite what their families said. But then waves of doubt flooded in to overwhelm him.

His thoughts lingered on Lark, looking for the signs of deepening intimacy in their time spent together. Was she a free agent, might his sentiments towards her be returned? Her troubles—would she be prepared to share them? Lark could be tetchy sometimes, but that was half the charm.

That moment she had peered down from the quayside—that face, her expression, the way she carried her head so the weight of her red hair fell to one side—Charlie wished to be in her life. He hoped there a mutual attraction. Maybe she desired security in marriage. Was he the marrying kind? And what had he to offer? All this emotion, he wasn't sure he liked it. Might it be in future tainted with recrimination and regret? He didn't know if he could carry the burden of someone else's happiness.

He moved across the bridge and waited outside the Custom House. It was one of her regular spots. A fair chance she'd show up soon. It would be harder to speak if he waited until the Floating Chapple.

A new paddle steam yacht turning in the middle of the river swirled the water. It churned like his stomach. An ear-splitting hoot from its horn disturbed a pair of swans and drowned out the seagulls' cries as they swooped in their quest for scraps. The air was pungent with the stink of engine oil and smoke as the great paddle wheel spun in a foaming dark wash.

Charlie spotted her at the other side of the bridge, crossing with a measured stride. His spirit sank when he saw who was behind her: Big Zander, William's lieutenant. Zander caught up and seized her by the arm, pulled her towards him. She twisted her face away when he held her by both shoulders and kissed her on the cheek before turning back the way he came.

She crossed the bridge, eyes on the ground. Charlie stepped out in front of her.

"We must speak."

She stopped and glanced up. Her eyes found his.

He stuttered, "I've m....missed you."

A wry smile curved her lips.

"And I need an honest answer. Are you with Zander now?"

Lark took a step back, examined him up and down. "Well, William has said I should be."

Charlie's face dropped, shoulders stooped, a knife in his heart.

"But, I've decided William can piss off. Had enough of him."

Charlie frowned, puzzled. "Then why are you kissing Zander on the street? As if selling yourself to satisfy your brother."

He caught a stab of pain and anger under her smoky eyelashes. "You dinnae know me sufficiently well to speak that way," snapped Lark. "Nothing happened."

His resentment flared, mirroring hers. Charlie, with the prick of tears, turned aside, sensed her eyes on his back. He spun.

"He was exhibiting you as if you were his," he said, bitterness in his voice.

"William says I should marry him, keep it in the family."

Charlie looked at the ground. "Do you love him?"

"Naw."

"No? Are you lying to me?"

"I dinnae have any affection for him."

Charlie glanced up.

Lark smiled. "Not like I do for you."

Charlie's heart lurched. He took Lark by the hand and dragged her up the Custom House steps and pulled her behind one of the pillars. His fingers tingled at the sensation rippling through her body as his palms glided to hold her waist, could feel Lark's breath quicken as they moved to her shoulders. She lifted her hands and entwined her fingers with his.

"The mere suggestion of you and him together…" Charlie's mouth set hard.

"Do you really think this a wise plan?" said Lark.

"Nope."

"Good, I'd be concerned if you did."

Lark put a palm to his cheek and slapped him softly with a gleeful giggle. Then, as if in slow motion, their faces moved close and their lips met, a taste of honey.

A full ten minutes later, Charlie took her by the hand and danced down the stairs. They cut over the bridge and headed towards the docks and the Floating Chapple.

On the wharf at the Shore, a tired-looking old paddle ferry was taking on the last of the passengers. It blew its whistle, engines clunking, steam belching across the quayside. A middle-aged couple at the back of the queue laid down their baggage next to the gangplank. Together they stepped to the river's edge, leant over, and were violently sick.

14 Days Later

27. Fear Stalks the Close
Monday

Lark McColligan

The first sign in the Vinegar Close courtyard came when the eldest of the young McGregor lads from the attic threw up by the McColligans' stair door one afternoon. That evening, Mrs McCurdy, the lady upstairs who sold bootlaces, said that two of her little ones had been sick when they arrived home from the Floating Chapple. There was a terrible mess, and she wondered if she could borrow some rags to mop it up. On the Thursday, four of the large family of Steinmans from across in Cherry Tree House fell ill.

Then the smell. Not only the stench expected from sickness and diarrhoea, but a musty, fishy stink. By the end of the first week, nine were sick in the yard, and now forty-eight. The niff got stronger as numbers increased until it might at times even overwhelm the odour from the river gas or the breweries when the wind blew it through the vennels.

At first, no one knew what it was or what to call it, or had the slightest idea for treating it. It started with a bout of severe sickness and putrid stools on the first day. Those affected just shrivelled up over the next two or three, eyes moving deeper into their sockets, then sunken cheeks before taking on a blue hue before death.

Flossie resolved to do all she could. She scrubbed her walls in vinegar, took herbs that Grannie O'Malley collected and smouldered them over a flame in a small dish. But the next Wednesday, wee Eliza started being sick, and by Saturday she was dead along with twenty-three others in the McColligans' courtyard.

It was soon in nearly every dwelling the length of Vinegar Close. It came for the big family of Mulligans in the shanty shacks behind Cherry Tree House. There were fourteen of them crammed into their hut the previous Friday, but only seven by the following.

The walls of the Vinegar Close courtyard today reverberated with screams, wails and moans. People talked about it being a plague. Grannie O'Malley and Tin Pan Aggie rarely left their regular seat on the steps of Cherry Tree House. Auld Grannie was always keen to share her wisdom. Now, others often joined them, eager to escape from their cramped, damp, crowded homes around the yard and get out into the air, no matter the weather. Grannie O'Malley stood puffing on her pipe, each belch of smoke followed by a hacking cough.

"Naw, naw it's no the plague," she said dismissively. "I remember that when I was a wee lassie, lots of folk died as well, but this yin's different."

"How so?" said Mrs McFarlane.

"I can tell you it bears no resemblance, unusual symptoms. You're no so likely to vomit if you have the plague, but this is pure fetid. The plague didnae stink half so bad."

"So, what is it?"

"Well, if you ask me, there was nowt to gain fae encouraging so many foreigners to live among us, so it's probably because of all the incomers. There's all sorts in the port. Frenchies, Blacks, Spanish, not to mention the Jews, Irish and Highlanders and the other useless, undeserving scroungers."

"Lazy bunch of wasters they are," said Tin Pan Aggie. "It's ridiculous, us official beggars cannae get a look in." She held out her lapel. "And this beggar's badge we got fae the Kirk Session is worthless nowadays."

"But half of the folk in our yard are Highlanders or Irish. In fact, is O'Malley not an Irish name?" said Mrs McFarlane.

Old Grannie O'Malley looked insulted. She pulled her shawl tighter round her head and moved her puny frame right under Mrs McFarlane's face. She stank of wet wool and tobacco. She glared up her large hooked nose, hacked, and then spat.

"Well, it may be something from the supernatural that we cannae explain," she hissed. "But more likely it's a judgment of oor Lord because of all the gambling and hooring that goes on in this port."

"But it's not only in Leith, it's around the entire country. Down south, too," said Mrs McFarlane.

Tin Pan Aggie's brow narrowed, thoughtful. "Or else it might be Burke and Hare all over again. Might be them doctors up in the Kirkgate needing bodies to chop up for their work. Bunch of warlocks. If you ask me, they should string them up, the lot of them. They even have a guard at the churchyards to stop the body snatchers, and we ken they all work for the quacks."

"Aye," said Grannie. "That new young minister at the Kirk said exactly that last week. Likely the Devil carries his mark on this, and whether it's the doctors or immigrants or beggars, it don't matter—it's Satan wha is to blame."

By the end of the month: forty-eight local cases, all but five dead. Posters had popped up at every corner of every street, and though few could read, they soon recognised the word "cholera".

Today, Lark and Flossie had avoided the steps and the courtyard. Lark had always thought death was only for other people. Neighbours had always died, be it with scarlet fever or consumption, but wee Eliza had seemed so strong and taken so quick. Withered away over a few days. Lark and Flossie had sat with her, helpless. The reaper now come to the McColligans' door.

That morning, the family had carried Eliza to the South Leith churchyard, lucky they could sell the silver necklace William said he'd found and avoid a pauper's burial. Images flitted through Lark's mind of Eliza taking her first unsteady steps. Gurgling cries of delight as she tottered over to hug Lark's knees. Her tousled curly hair and dimpled cheeks. Her squeals of joy as Lark spun her round by an arm and leg. She hadn't appreciated her in her nine short years. Now she knew she had lost a friend, a soulmate.

The bare wooden coffin was laid across two lengths of rope and hung suspended before being lowered jerkily by the diggers into the grave, the churchman already striding off, having mumbled a few words. Lark lifted a handful of soil and stood at the grave's edge, let it trickle through her fingers and bounce on the homemade coffin, before turning away, eyes hot with tears. She quivered as the diggers lifted their spades. Wee Eliza, alone and cold in the ground.

Lark trembled, had been feverish since she woke. They left the gravestones and headed home. A wave of weariness swept over her, energy gone. Struggling to keep up, she felt faint, sweat streaming. Lark wiped her hand across her forehead, stopping to rest against a low wall. Flossie turned and noticed, and retraced her steps.

"Are you all right?"

"I'm fine," Lark said, before leaning over the wall and vomiting.

She groaned. Flossie caught her arm as she slumped.

"William, Andy, come back!" shouted Flossie, fear in her voice.

Lark fell to her knees.

"She's ill. We need to get her home, help me carry her."

William stepped forward, then hesitated. "Ach, no way—she's covered in puke and shite."

"William," snapped Flossie; she bared her teeth. "Lift her."

William noted the expression in his mother's eye. "Ach," then mutterings.

He lifted Lark over his shoulder and strode for home.

28. Angus Gets a Lead
Tuesday

Superintendent Andrew Angus

Superintendent Angus arrived home late and rose early. He winced as he sat to breakfast, rump still tender. A thin smile at the memory— Arabella's sessions always lifted his spirits. So different in comparison to Bunty's incessant carping, and it was a joy to spend time with one so angelic and trustworthy, who took a real interest in his difficulties at work.

Yesterday, not only had there been more cholera deaths, but he'd heard more whisky had gone. A substantial shipment waiting on the West Dock, and over a handful of night-time hours, it had vanished. Of course, no witnesses, or at least none prepared to come forward, always with big stuff. Apart from a spate of muggings, the petty crime around the port had decreased over the past month, despite the impoverished beggars. But not a week passed without a major theft. Crates of spices, barrels of whisky, pallets of wine bottles, bolts of cloth, sacks of sugar or lengths of timber, and yet he didn't have a clue who was behind it. Clearly, they were organised, but having lost his best snitches, he was at a loss. He pulled his hands through his hair in frustration.

He flipped through his notebook on the kitchen table over a cup of tea, boiled egg and bread, glad to have time and space to review his cases. Despite copious notes, he had never resolved the mahogany robbery at Ramage's yard, and now had pages of observations on other thefts, not to mention the murder of his informants. He mulled over the growing list. What had he missed? He drummed his fingers on the dinner table, toyed with his shirt cuff Had he missed a connection somewhere?

Dawn broke, the light from the window grew.

"Oooh, Daddy," said Esmeralda, his youngest, at the kitchen door. "Haven't seen you for ages."

"Daddy's been busy, sweetheart," Angus whispered. "Catching wicked men."

"Look," said Esmeralda. "We got Mother a birthday gift with the money you gave us."

She held up a handsome large silk handkerchief embroidered with delicate pink flowers in the corner, and the initials: BA. Esmeralda pointed. "See? Mother's initials: Bunty Angus."

Mmmm, something clicked in his mind. He flicked back a few pages. So driven to track down the stolen timber, hadn't made the link at the time. Realised he should have.

That handkerchief he'd seen young Reverend Ponsonby buying at Archie McTavish's shop. He remembered the initials: AP. Same as taken from the banker Alexander Preston when assaulted and robbed. Quite a coincidence that Archie was selling such a handkerchief.

He mused a moment. Possibly nothing, but needed exploring. Any chance of getting anything on that scoundrel Archie McTavish was well worth pursuing.

'Visit Rev Ponsonby' he scribbled in the notebook.

"Andrew, Andrew!" screeched Bunty's voice from upstairs. "Andrew, is that you? Are you there?"

Superintendent Angus stood up, stroked Esmeralda's curls, stuffed his mouth with the last of the egg and bread, crossed the kitchen and slipped out the back door.

***

As the afternoon light faded, a near calamitous error was made.

Arabella thought it prudent not to rush. Best wait until after dark, but not too late. An important customer was visiting her rooms later that night, so it would be wise to not linger here too long.

Utmost discretion was required. The important man on the floor at her feet, once word got out, would cause quite a hullabaloo. The minister at the town's United Succession Church was well respected, so best she vanish. And for this to happen in his own church at the Chapple of Ease… Embarrassing for the poor chap, but he shouldn't have tried to swindle the wrong people.

She was rarely one for metaphors, but on this occasion, tears were flowing like a river as the life sucked out of him, his fat face contorted in agony, gasping for air. Messier than a knife. She felt a shiver of nostalgia for her younger days in France. A blade was more efficient if used well, and more straightforward than all this messing about leading him on for weeks, but Mr Black had insisted.

Like most males, he was so pliable when offered a chance of forbidden sex. They would move mountains, sniffing around like dogs. Only natural, she supposed. We are only animals, after all.

It was always almost disappointingly easy. Engineer a meeting on the street and catch a glance, raise her beautiful eyes and hold their gaze for just a second too long before lowering them again, and they were hooked. Then, over two or three weeks, arrange further encounters until everything was as it needed to be.

Insist on a clandestine liaison on the gentleman's own turf; they would always acknowledge the wisdom of ensuring total privacy and utmost discretion. With that established, she'd demand he arrange a sumptuous private dinner first, just the two of them, with a promise of heavenly delights, and would insist that she supply the fine wine.

"I'm in love with you," had been the final words spoken before the toxin kicked in to close off his throat and take the power from his legs.

Poetic that it should end this way, with him rolling on the floor with his trousers round his ankles, the waxy, puffy, entitled face now a vivid shade of purple, like an overripe beetroot. As a minister of one of the best attended churches in town, he had become famous for his pulpit rants on the Sabbath, often against women such as her. "Jezebel" ranked among his favourite words preached from the high pulpit.

He looked pathetic in his death throes, fat neck straining at his dog collar, his delicate, small hands clawing at it. The fine Geneva gown, his pulpit robe riding up the pot belly, spindly legs wriggling like an upturned beetle.

Earned a good fee, and there was a certain beauty in it. In this case, the stupid man had encouraged his parishioners to invest in the fund he organised for the poor.

"Jesus himself would have given generously," he'd spouted in last week's sermon.

Though Arabella had discovered the needy had received not a farthing. His flock would likely be unhappy when the truth came to light. Normally, Mr Black only used Arabella's services to dispose of secretive police informers or other such rogues who operated in the shadows, but this was a special case. It was unfortunate for the minister on the floor that on Mr Black's (who had always been a keen churchgoer) occasional visits to Leith, the United Succession Church was the very congregation that he had chosen to join.

She left him in his private apartments above the nave as darkness settled. Slipped down the stairs, aiming to creep out the back entrance. She knew he had ensured the church was empty, but as she arrived at the bottom of the steps, she heard a door at the rear creak open. Footsteps. Arabella moved to the shadows and kept perfectly still. The footsteps moving upstairs, she stole to the side entrance and reached for the door handle. A piercing scream sounded up above.

"Murder, murder!"

Arabella's stomach lurched, the body discovered. They must not see her. Move fast.

She slipped out the exit and into the back lane. The wynd was ragged in the gloom, empty, streaked with soundless shadows from the few shining windows in the ill-lit thoroughfare. She crept away, taking occasional glances behind to ensure she wasn't being followed.

Her heart raced as she took the long way round to her apartment off Burgess Lane. Relief coursed through her on her safe arrival, and the door clicked shut. She opened the window and breathed slow and deep, hands trembling, relieved that her work in the town was near complete. Soon, it would be time to return home.

Late that night, Lord Haddington gingerly caressed his bottom before making his goodbyes. Satisfied, but expression unchanged, the usual aristocratic sneer as he pulled his hat over his eyes and left with a nod.

She leant her forehead on the closed door and sighed. What a day. She still felt tense after her close escape at the church. Mr Black had informed her he had achieved the required level of control in the port, so she was now free to move back to Marseilles. He would soon delegate authority for the town to a designated underling, and he'd promised to join her back home later. Mr Black had already selected; Arabella had met him, a Mr Adam White, soon to be town Provost. His large rump had made an easy target and he had squealed like a pig, but she had total confidence in Mr Black's judgement, so he must be an ideal choice, with the necessary contacts in the world of business.

For her, this place was too full of complicated memories. Once she had repaid the debt, she'd return to the continent.

Arabella hung the well-worn riding crop on its hook, then put on her nightgown before lying on the bed, a little breathless after such a vigorous session with His Lordship. She giggled at how that crusty-faced aristocrat had told her he was in the Scots Greys at the Battle of Waterloo and still had shrapnel from a French musket ball in his buttocks.

"The poor old chap won't be able to sit for a week," she said, and chuckled.

Arabella was careful with the amount she used, but following a day like today she had earned a little treat. She turned to the bedside dresser, removed the two pounds seven shillings and sixpence Haddington had placed in the dish and put it in her purse. She twisted the key in the drawer underneath, revealing the pair of similar boxes. From the smaller, with its delicate red dragon mother-of-pearl design, she lifted the object, turned it in her hand. It glinted in the candlelight. She polished it with a soft cloth before returning it to its box. A shame to see it go, had a sentimental attachment after so many years. But it would be disrespectful to her past and she would have let herself down if she did not return it to its rightful owner.

The second box, with a blue-green pattern of delicate leaves. Her hand trembled before she opened it. Over the years, she'd shared its contents with a strange assortment of others, from Bible-thumping preachers to sad soldiers, pernickety policemen and sleekit cutthroats, timid matrons and maddened mariners. But whether alone or within the secret lives of that collection of liars, flatterers, chancers, crooks and two-faced backstabbers, the effects were always the same.

Inside, the objects lay on the blue silk lining. She removed them one by one. A needle with a bamboo stem and metal tip, a thin long-handled spoon, a miniature knife, and a small sandalwood box with a carved design. From the second drawer underneath, she lifted a lacquered object. Beautiful craftsmanship, painted with a snake pattern—a pipe with a long, thin stem and a miniature bowl at one end.

Arabella opened the sandalwood box and picked up the mud-coloured substance. Bengal's very best. With the knife, she shaved the tiniest piece and placed it with care in the spoon's bowl. She lifted it over the candle flame until the gummy material melted into a liquid.

With the ceremonial air of an ancient pagan ritual, Arabella dipped the needle tip in the now sizzling bubble and transferred it to the pipe's bulb, put the stem to her lips and drew in thick, oily smoke. She held her breath before exhaling, then repeated the whole process once more.

She thought briefly about all the men who had been in her life. The ones she loved, the ones she hated—she still had the scars from her father. The rich ones, the poor ones, the dead ones. But with this, other people were not required. She could rest here all day and feel accepted, appreciated, loved. With no desire to think about her own history either. All those men…

Thoughts drifted away. No need to delve into the past.

Soon she was light as a feather, floating on a cloud. Gravity lessened, every muscle drained of any tightness or tension. Did she even exist? Yet her mind was nimble and clear, a world of visions, dreams, shapes and graphic colour. Like the deepest sleep, yet at her most awake. A muted existence with absolutely no desire.

To her sharp mind came one brief thought: what if tomorrow starts without me?

An awareness of things to do, people to see—but not now. Tomorrow.

29. Charlie Finds a Way
Wednesday

Dr Thomas Latta

Charlie lay back and sighed, watching the slow-moving clouds above. It was as if he had pinned his hopes and dreams on them, though it must have been a windy day.

For the first week after the Custom House steps, they'd been together here three times. The following week, it had been every day apart from the Wednesday. Then they'd met the day before her wee sister's funeral.

They should have met again yesterday, but she didn't show. Charlie had come back today in case she'd made a mistake with the days.

Charlie lay in their secret little spot on the sands, a shallow dip among the dunes, protected from the wind at the far end of the links. The dipping sun told how late it was. She wasn't coming. He'd never imagined it ending this way, in this spot, their private haven hidden from William and his gang.

On their way here for the first time, Lark had identified another fine spot: the ropery buildings stretched along the coast past the Glassworks. They'd found a neuk where the workers gathered on their break to smoke. "A new source to be mined in future," announced Lark with her infectious laugh, joyful at the excellent discovery.

Today, Charlie had brought a roll of grubby canvas and splashed out all he had on a picnic. On the Shore he'd purchased a bottle from the Britannia Inn and a couple of yesterday's biscuits from Crawford's Bakery.

Over the past fortnight, they'd often leaned against each other here, watched ships coming and going along at the harbour mouth.

Their relationship had blossomed over the past couple of weeks. Lark would sit with her head on his shoulder. She let him stroke the back of her neck or gently caress her hands, especially the one missing a pinkie. Or he'd kiss her forearms and neck, mouth exploring, long soft kisses on her hair and cheeks. Then lean forward and brush her lips, her breasts on his chest, breath quicker, would press his mouth to hers, touching tongues, her hips pressed into his, a beautiful pain, then a look from those eyes, feel flushed, hot even. She would close them and he'd kiss her delicate lids. One unseasonably warm afternoon they'd even gone in the water in their shirts and underwear, then ran up the beach and lain baking on the sand with wet clothes sticking to them until they dried.

That smile, those freckles creased across her nose. It lit up his world. Or the way she moved. She held herself with a precise balance. The perfect shape of her calf, above which he might have liked to explore further. Or that hair. When the sun was behind her, it was like strands of golden thread. And none of that giggling stuff, a serious girl. Tough and at times tetchy, but gorgeous and fun.

Today, a graceful, fast smack from the London and Edinburgh shipping company pulled from the harbour.

"Only takes a couple days if the wind's right," he had once told her. "Faster than a steamer, and wind's free. Coal costs a fortune."

Men were at the braces and halyards, others strung out along its great yards, ready to release the sails, immense stretches of canvas that snapped into the breeze. But sail was giving way to steam. A big steamer coming the other direction churned through the water with its vast paddles plunging, looking as a giant noisy warrior, the wind having no effect other than to send the smoke from its funnel, be it to the east, west, north or south.

Lark and he had discussed going on a voyage one day, an adventure, maybe America or France. Neither had any idea where these places were but it sounded an exciting idea, though they'd concluded not to leave their mothers for now. Though Lark had said that while she knew lots of things—how to sell stuff, how to test an apple's freshness by tapping it in the right spot, a few reading letters, how to sew and how to make gruel—knowing so little about much else sometimes made her feel ill.

Charlie used to think people wanted to know too much, they all wanted too many answers, but now he realised he did as well.

Over the last couple of weeks, Lark had rarely been from his thoughts. He dreamt of her every night. Some mornings woke with stains on his blanket.

But no sign of her today. How could he have got it so wrong? Charlie was in love. It had never been said, but he now realised it should have been. He would never be interested in other women. He needed someone who wanted him, hoped and prayed that person might be her. Might she have changed her mind? He couldn't believe it. He would be lost.

She wasn't coming. It was going to break his heart.

He wanted her to be here now, so he could tell her what was in his head. That he didn't wish to be unburdened and free, and alone. He had fallen for her that time she looked down from the quayside on the Shore; he didn't want to be with anyone else, neither did he want any of these barrow boys or apprentices hanging around. He would tell her that in future it might go wrong—usually does between Prestons and McColligans—but their families might come around. He never wanted to lose her; she was the only good thing in his life. Without her, everything in future would be tainted by her memory. If only she could get inside his head to see what was there. He needed to confess all this to her face.

Charlie dreamed of the two of them laughing against the world.

There was only one thing to do. He finished the bread and beer, stood, rolled the canvas and hid it under a whin bush. He prayed they would share it next time.

Charlie headed back along the sands as the first drops of rain fell, before making for the Yardheads. He waited until dark. He steeled himself, ready for trouble.

From Giles Street, he dared a glance into Vinegar Close, the narrow lane quiet. The clouds thickened. Thin rain and a cool gusty breeze spiralled through the lanes and vennels, lit by a full moon. He peered around the corner before moving towards the McColligans' courtyard. William strolled out in his stovepipe hat, right in front of him.

William grinned like a cat that had cornered a mouse. Charlie had met William like this often in his dreams, during which he had punched, strangled and stabbed him, and enjoyed it every time.

"Preston."

"Where is she, McColligan?"

"Whit's it to you?"

"Whit's happened?"

"You're not going anywhere near her, Preston. Wha do you think you are, strolling into my patch making demands? Expect it's time I taught you a lesson."

Charlie's heart turned cold. This time it was for real. William made to come at him, but catching him wrongfooted, Charlie thrust forward and grabbed him by the lapels of his tailcoat.

"I said, where is she!"

William pushed him away. "Fuck off, Preston."

Charlie stood his ground, fists raised. "You're going nowhere until you've telt me."

William's mouth formed a wolfish grin. "Oooh, lover boy, think you might have left it too late. It's a shame, Preston, had proper plans for that lassie—would be worth a pretty penny—but no chance for that now."

Charlie's anger flared, chin jutting. "What do you mean? You were going to sell her, your own sister?" he said, horror etched on taut lips.

"Wouldn't you like to ken? Making money, not something you understand. Stick to grovelling in the mud, that's all you're good for."

Charlie sensed a red mist come down. He swung with his right and caught William a glancing blow on the jaw. A wild swing with his left. Missed, now exposed. William responded with a sharp jab to the ribs.

"I said, where is she!" screamed Charlie, stepping back.

William laughed. "Well, I was going to sell her, but too late for that, Preston. She's got the cholera, is turning blue as we speak."

Charlie made a wild lunge, veins flooding with adrenalin. William deflected the charge. Charlie blocked William's right hook. His arm shot out and whacked William hard on the side of the head, sending him careening against the wall. William scraped along the facade, his face taut, drew out a knife and swung. Sound of tearing as the blade ripped Charlie's shirt. Charlie danced backwards, avoided the slash. William gave an involuntary shudder at the glint in Charlie's eye.

Charlie kicked out at William's leg, knocking him off balance, sent him reeling back against the wall. In a flash he was upon him. Grabbed his wrist with the knife and twisted; the dagger dropped, then two uppercuts to the chin, both connecting. William's head thrown back, sending him stumbling. Charlie tried to grapple, but William was too quick and slipped from his grasp. He ran, leaving Charlie clutching at thin air.

Charlie's chased for a few steps. "Aye, not so hard when you've no backup, ya coward."

He took a deep breath, kicked the knife into a drain and turned into the McColligans' courtyard. Didn't break his stride when the lumbering Big Zander stepped out from the gloom. Zander looked Charlie hard in the eye, didn't like what he saw, and backed away. Charlie pushed past him and hammered on the McColligans' door.

Flossie answered, eyes puffy red.

"Lark," said Charlie.

"She's dying," whispered Flossie, and her face crumpled.

Charlie shoved past her. "I ken someone wha can help."

Flossie stood frozen on the spot, her only response a sob. Charlie crouched and lifted Lark from her bed, carried her out the door and headed straight for the Kirkgate.

"Ah, young love," said Grannie O'Malley as they passed. "Awfy complicated these days, was much simpler back in oor day."

"Huh, young folk nowadays," said Tin Pan Aggie, turning up her nose. "Carrying folk aboot like a sack o' tatties. It's ridiculous whit they get up tae."

***

Dr Latta sat at his desk with his head in his hands. It was getting late. He'd been on from six, would have to sleep soon. Rubbed his eyes. One last effort; he turned and picked what he needed from the shelves of glass and earthenware bottles and jars untidily arranged on the wall behind. Pushed back his hair, lifted the pencil from the table once again, and opened the notebook. He decided to start from the beginning, rechecking his calculations for the hundredth time.

"I'm so close," he said in a whisper under his breath. "It's only a question of finding the correct salt solutions in the correct combination."

He hunched over his desk, deep in concentration. The answer was in front of him; he just needed to look hard enough. There were signs and clues in the mass of information he had accumulated. All his calculations, previous recipes tried, prior failed attempts—he just needed to piece it together. It required a different approach, an answer not based on the usual alcohol or opium. Time to think outside of the box. It wasn't as simple as just finding a stimulant or a sedative; it had to be a natural phenomenon with a natural solution.

The problem, of course, was that some people were looking for divine intervention or miracles, to turn metal into gold, but that's not how it worked. What mattered was careful observation. How are substances made, what happens if you add other substances, how do they change, what happens when you add heat, or water, what then changes, what happens when you remove impurities? Observation, not magic. Though people were still dying. Try to turn theory into reality, make it happen. Salt and water to replace the blood, might it work? He ground the mortar and pestle, measured and poured and measured again as he sought the correct proportions of potassium, sodium bicarbonate and chloride to place in the porcelain saucers.

The church clock struck ten. It had been a long week, on call day and night, a responsibility he shared with three of his colleagues at the dispensary. Together with this team, he knew they made a difference. With a great deal of cajoling, they'd convinced the authorities to cancel public gatherings, try to clean the poorer housing, ban the markets and shut the factories despite the outcry from the owners. Although they didn't know the cause of the illness, they were convinced that these measures helped slow the spread.

After working for twenty minutes more, he'd prepared the salts for the next patient, whenever they came. He stood and stretched. Time for sleep. Wouldn't go home tonight, just flop here a few hours. Tomorrow he'd get home and remove the stench of chlorine from his hands and change his shirt. The stink of cholera, that smell of death, cloying and still detectable under the odour of the vinegar used to counteract it.

A sudden loud kick on the door, then a second time. Latta opened it, eyes wide.

"You said if you could ever repay me," blurted the boy.

He stood with a girl in his arms, a shrivelled bundle.

Latta stared in surprise. "You..."

"Help her."

"You're the boy who saved me from being robbed."

"Can you save her?" cried the boy.

There was desperation in his eyes. Latta stood aside to let them in.

"Bring her in, lay her on the bed."

"She's dying."

"We can only do what we can do."

Working fast, Latta added spoonfuls from the dishes of prepared salts into individual pint bottles, filled them with water, and gave a vigorous shake.

"Bring me that contraption," he said, pointing to a wheeled trolley where sat a metal bowl, in which stood a long metal cylinder with a plunger handle at the top.

Latta attached a flexible tube to a narrow opening at the bottom of the long cylinder. The boy looked on, mesmerised. To the other end of the tube, Latta fitted a very fine goose quill. Then, with care, stabbed it into the girl's arm.

"Whit's that for?" said the boy.

"Replacing essential salts."

"Whit are essential salts?"

"Quiet," said Latta.

Latta filled the metal cylinder with the first pint of his solution and slowly depressed the handle above. The cylinder's contents were pushed into the girl's vein. He stopped, pulled back her eyelids and studied, placed his fingers on her wrist.

The boy considered his expression, which gave nothing away, Latta's eyes darting and cautious, watching for any effect.

"Has it worked?" asked the boy.

Latta raised his tired eyes. "What's your name?"

"Charlie Preston."

"You can help me, Charlie. Put your fingers gently here." He lifted Lark's wrist. "What do you feel?"

Charlie concentrated. "It's the tiniest movement, almost nothing."

"That is what's known as the pulse. It's the blood flowing through the body. I need you to concentrate hard and tell me if anything changes."

Latta filled the cylinder with a second pint and again, a gentle push of the plunger on top. Charlie kept his fingers on the girl's wrist. Nothing changed. His face fell. An hour crept by as Doctor Latta continued with his task.

After the fourth pint—

"Her pulse," said Charlie. "I sense something."

Latta stopped and took the girl's wrist. He used his shirt to wipe his brow and refilled the metal cylinder with the fifth pint.

"Let's keep going, Charlie."

The doctor pushed the handle until the fifth pint was gone.

"It's fuller," said Charlie, struggling to keep the excitement out of his voice. "It's firmer, and her breathing, its less laboured."

Latta said nothing, eyes tight with concentration. The sixth pint went in, and Charlie's anxious expression changed. He stared open-mouthed. The girl opened her eyes and smiled.

"Charlie," she whispered, a quiet croak.

Latta spoke, but Charlie didn't hear. He was too busy listening to his heart sing.

30. Archie at Leisure
Thursday

Archie McTavish

For Fat Archie, Thursday night was rat night. Along with whisky, ale and Mr Roberts' best meat pies, there were many other entertainments and purchases to be made at the Stinking Pig. Through the main door he found the spartan bar, black roof beams and the smell of a cauldron of pork stew. Open twenty-four hours, ignoring the cholera restrictions, and full of the usual sailors, tradesman, prostitutes, adventurers, gangsters, gamblers, beggars and various other human debris that washed up on its shores, its principal attraction on a cold evening that it was the only place with light or heat, sometimes even hot water.

Roberts, the landlord, a broad, sly-looking fellow with biceps like pistons (upon one, three scars in a neat row) had never gone in for the ornate wood and brass fittings becoming popular in the town's more upmarket establishments.

In the basement, the rat pit. When Archie and Bluebell arrived, there were already the yaps of other dogs ready to test their qualities. The usual array of customers from every level of society. Coils of smoke rose from cigars and pipes of men standing around the bar, drinking and speaking of betting odds and dogs. A big swarthy fellow with nervous eyes held a small dog under his arm, a surly-faced bulldog. A scrawny boy in an oversized, patched coachman's blue greatcoat held a highland terrier that strained at its leash, having smelt the rats and keen to get started. Sleeping in his owner's arms like a baby, a Skye terrier, while a growling white bull terrier with a piratical black patch over one eye sat at the feet of a morose, tall man in a smart waistcoat and knee breeches. Archie's Bluebell appeared more interested in the smell of Mr Roberts' pies than any rats.

The room was low-roofed, smoky and bare, a fire in the grate, beside which was placed the most comfortable-looking chair, where sat Mr Roberts' own dog, 'The Butcher'. A huge bulldog with a scarred face like a battered, worn boxing glove, he yawned and looked bored. On one wall were dog collars adorned with rings and buckles, prizes Butcher had earned over the years.

"How many tonight?" said Archie.

"Plenty," said Mr Roberts. "Busy ferrets this week."

The crowd moved from the bar to the pit, Archie in the best seat, a small private box. The rest of the audience filled the benches or hung over the side or else stood on chairs at the rear. William arrived. Archie nodded to the seat behind, and William sat. On a shelf above the arena were three stuffed dogs who were famous in their day, including Archie's last terrier, Jumper.

William leaned forward. "You said you had another job for me."

"You see that dug up there?" said Archie. "The best yin I ever had. I watched her kill a dozen rats as big as herself." A tear welled in Archie's eye. "The toll of too many bites did her in, poisoned. If I kent then whit I ken now, would never have worked her so hard. But this here, little Bluebell, is her daughter. She's good, but not as good. Jumper once killed three hundred rats in five and a half minutes, stands as the record for the Stinking Pig and unlikely ever bettered."

William studied the stuffed animal but said nothing. By now every space around the pit was filled. Costermongers in corduroy suits, Lord Haddington's footman still wearing his livery, ships' officers slurring with their tunics unbuttoned, and various tradesmen, carpenters, tailors, hammermen and shoemakers with their best frock coats slipped over working clothes.

The crowd was becoming impatient for the match to start, but Mr Roberts didn't hurry. He moved round the room handling each of the hounds with his expert eye, feeling their paws, studying their eyes. Two assistants entered, carrying a wide cage full of a seething mass of rats. The dogs sparked into life, barking and whining. Archie gripped Bluebell's collar as she tried to jump the wall. Above the pit, a circle eight feet across with wooden surround, half a dozen oil lamps lit the white painted floor.

"Now, William," whispered Archie, "you telt me last week you were having troubles with your sister."

William frowned, eyes dark. "That wee cow."

Mr Roberts dug his hands into the cage, lifted a rat by the tail and threw it into the pit. The dogs barked louder as another twenty rats followed.

"Place your bets, gentlemen." Mr Roberts' assistant moved around the room, collecting money and recording wagers.

By now, the rats were scurrying round the circle, some on hind legs cleaning mouths with little paws, others unsuccessfully searching for a nook or cranny in which to hide.

"First up, the novices," shouted Mr Roberts.

"It's a scam," whispered Archie. "Roberts already kens the likely result."

A heavy, swarthy man threw a grumpy-looking bulldog into the pit. The other dogs responded in a rising crescendo of whining. Once the dog had landed, he stood still and sniffed the air, though appeared as if he wasn't particularly interested in the rats, now clustered together.

"Wha does she think she is, bloody lassie telling me what to do, four-fingered wee witch," said William, snarling. "She needs to watch herself. She shows me no respect and has a big mouth."

"Watch, gentlemen," said the swarthy man. "My little Tommy, he's a real good yin."

"Looks like it's never seen a rodent in his life," laughed a jolly-faced, drunk sailor with an enormous belly.

The hound's owner screamed at the beast and banged the pit's side. The bulldog moved forward towards the group. A rat sprang forward and attacked his nose; the dog drew back, astonished. He shook off the rat and plunged his snout into the heap and lifted his head with one clenched in his jaws, but it curled around his nose, squealing. The swarthy man had to shout "Drop it" several times until he did.

"Oh dear, doesnae sound like you two are getting on," said Archie.

The first dog was withdrawn and the white Skye terrier thrown in. She picked up an already dead rat and ignored the living. She shook it with vigour, the rat's head thumping the floor in a steady rhythm.

"Ha ha!" shouted the drunk, jolly sailor. "She's good a shaking dead uns, but what about the live uns?"

"And I hear she is recovering from the cholera."

"Aye, that lanky shit Charlie Preston slipped past oor guards yesterday and took her to some doctor."

"Ah," said Archie. "Preston and a McColligan, always likely end in tears."

"Ach, I cannae be doing with mouthy wimmin," said William. "And she seems to have taken a fancy to him. Skinny bastard's been hanging around oor ground. Not likely he's getting away with that. The boys are keeping an eye oot and have already chased him twice now. We are onto him."

There was a pause as Mr Roberts entered the ring and announced the evening's main event. The few dead rats were cleared, the cage returned. Mr Roberts put his hand in, withdrawing over fifty others by the tail until the pit filled.

"Only big yins," he declared.

The creatures scurried around wildly before gathering themselves in a swirling mound running halfway up the wall on one side of the pit. It was clear these were sewer rats; the stink that filled the room was that of an open cesspit.

"Well, that's good news she is on the mend. Your maw will be delighted."

"Aye, I suppose she is."

The bull terrier was now stretching his neck, his mouth foaming in excitement, the morose man holding him struggling to keep control. Mr Roberts lifted the beast, attached a rope around its collar and hooked it to the inside edge of the pit. The dog appeared to be strangling itself in a mad frenzy to get at the seething mound.

"Set the clock," shouted Roberts.

He freed the bull terrier, and it charged towards the writhing mass.

"All a bit of a dilemma for you, William, my lad, but what can I say, women are women. They all get hysterical from time to time. They dinnae think rationally like us men. But anyway, to business, I've got another job for you, and this one pays extra."

William looked up, interest in his eyes. The terrier charged forward and, with a growl, pushed his nose into the rat mound and brought one up in its jaws.

"I have a customer, has asked me to provide for him. An older lassie this time. He happens to have spotted her and has taken a liking. So, crossed my mind, we may do a wee bit business and offer a service to my client, in the usual fashion."

"When?"

"Delivery on Tuesday night."

William looked up, a grim smirk. "If she is older, I want more than usual. No so easy as some scrawny wee orphan. She might fight like a cat."

"She won't if you do it right." Archie took out the bottle of dwale and passed it behind. "Only requires a drink of this and you shouldn't have problems."

They agreed the fee.

"Stop the clock," exclaimed Roberts.

William smiled a satisfied smile and pocketed the jar. By now, around two dozen rats with broken necks and bloody heads were staining the pit floor. Others quivered in their death throes, the terrier struggling with the last one, which clung squealing to his nose until he dashed the life out of it against the pit wall.

"Here is the usual advance, full payment when the job's completed," said Archie. He passed silver. "Come back tomorrow and I'll give you the lassie's name and delivery address. Now, on your way, I've other business to attend. I've an important date on Saturday."

"Twenty-three in four minutes," shouted Roberts.

"Off you go," said Archie. "Now it's Bluebell's turn. Occasionally failure is unavoidable, yet tonight, I believe she will give that big Butcher a run for his money."

***

Well after midnight, Archie climbed the stairs past the still-raucous ground-floor bar and up to the first landing. Here, Mr Roberts kept rooms for private business away from the prying eyes and ears of the authorities. The Stinking Pig had in the past given the magistrates cause for concern, a suspicion that anywhere the poor could gather in their own social space might, if left to fester, lead to crime or political dissent.

When Archie had completed his task, he stood back and checked the table was set to his satisfaction. He added the final touch to the centre, the bunch of begonias—perfect. Archie stepped back to admire his work, set for tomorrow. Him and Flossie together at last. He would tell her what he had wanted to say for years. And that mother-of-pearl box with the red dragon design, he might even get an inkling of what happened to it. After all, he had paid Earnest Preston a large deposit in advance.

31. The Session Reacts to the Crisis
Friday

The Kirk Session

Mr Alexander Preston, financial adviser to the group, leant back in his chair, saying nothing. The emergency Kirk Session meeting had turned a little heated.

"Absolute drivel," said Lord Haddington in his aristocratic drawl.

The sagging face of Commissioner White reddened before responding. "How can you advocate such a thing, sir? Conditions in the town have now become frightful. The pestilence is sweeping everything before it; neither age, nor gender, nor even your station in life will guarantee escape. There's terrible consternation among the people. All manufactories and workshops are closed, business at a standstill, women in a state of distraction, rushing in every direction for medical help for their dying husbands, husbands for their wives, and children for their parents."

"Pah," said Haddington. "You're only seeing the bad of it. I suggest not to lose heart in such dark times; things can't keep going the same way forever."

In the chair was the Right Reverend McIntosh, lime-sour lips creasing his wizened face. "Oh, cholera," he cried, clasping his palms as if in prayer. "It's a divine intervention, we are paying for our sins." He closed his eyes and pointed to the rafters. "Oh, you are my refuge and my fortress, my God, in whom I trust, for he will deliver us from the deadly pestilence."

"Amen." Heads around the table nodded.

"We have problems conveying the dead to the grave," said Deacon Johnston "I'm sorry for being brutally frank, but it's been a sair ficht for a half loaf.[6] The gravediggers are working without interruption both night and day; those Leithers who possess the means quit the

---

6   *It's a sair ficht for a half loaf (Scots proverb) – Life's hard, and often you only get half of what you expect in return for what you put in.*

town and fly for safety of the countryside, and those remaining see nothing before them but disease and death."

He paused, and with his sleeve wiped the permeant drip from his long red nose. "We lack burial space in the churchyards. The yards of the parish are full to overflowing. Today I noticed human remains strewn over the ground, and then there's the problem of body snatchers. We are being overwhelmed."

Young Ponsonby paused taking the minutes and interrupted. "This pestilence was sent by the Lord to punish our sins. Our world is wicked and the Lord fearsome, and he is angry." He swept his hand over the table. "You cannot hide from his justice. The only option is to pray, pray and pray."

Old Reverend McIntosh, fingered his pock-marked nose, then thumped the table. "Well said, Ponsonby. So, what's required is we humbly prostrate ourselves before the throne of the Almighty. The solution is in the scriptures."

"Humbug," Haddington said, his tone peevish. "Whatever will be will be."

Reverend McIntosh's voice trembled as he raised his finger to the heavens. "I will bring the sword upon you. I am the Lord; I have spoken. He who guides us in the storm and whose arm is mighty, we must beseech him to stay the hand of his avenging angel and to turn from our doors this escalating calamity."

"Absolute rubbish," exclaimed Haddington, now on his feet. "Any idiot can see that this disease affects the poor, the Highlanders and the Irish and the other scum who inhabit the slums of Yard Heads and St Anthony's. They are the real problem. It's clear they are inferior both physically and morally. Such displays of sermonising and prayer from yourselves are mere distraction."

"Yes," said Commissioner White, jowls quivering as he returned Haddington's derisive stare. "Thanks to the degrading and filthy conditions in which they live, subsisting on the scantiest of food and clad in misery with cloth of the worst description, then herded together in dark, ill-ventilated rooms. The Yardheads are an insanitary place of animal droppings, blubber-boiling dens, slaughterhouses and open, decaying sewers. Underneath the floorboards of their overcrowded cellars lurks a noxious sea of cesspits as old as the houses, and many rarely drained."

"Now look, you can sit there on your great bahookie pontificating as long as you like," said Haddington, red faced and pointing, "but you and your sort are all suffering from cholera phobia. It's complete humbug I say. All we need to do is cast out the beggars."

Commissioner White bristled at the personal insult. "Well, at least I don't have a beak like a parish pickaxe[7]."

Mr Preston, the banker, stood and flapped his arms. "Gentlemen, gentlemen, please can we be calm for a moment."

He waited until the grumbling stopped. Haddington and White glared at each other, lips twisted. Haddington sat, winced, and adjusted his position.

Preston continued, "The reality is we have achieved what we can. It may not be perfect, but it is better than if we did nothing. We closed some taverns and schools, cancelled meetings of the trade corporations and postponed weddings. Dr Latta and his colleagues prepared well when informed this pestilence was on the way. Houses in the Yardheads and Old Babylon have been cleaned, including the privies and some cesspools; they even whitewashed walls. The fact is we have done what's possible with the resources available—public health measures are in place to curtail its impact. We know the houses and living conditions of the impoverished are the likely reservoirs of disease; so many houses were cleansed and disinfected, food and bedding provided, some middens cleared. Dr Latta at the dispensary is providing direct treatment for many cases."

"Yes." Haddington gave a scoffing laugh. "We are well aware of that, but don't you realise that to whitewash only one of their abodes costs four shillings. Four shillings, I say. So who will pay? That's what I crave to know. The poor box is empty, and we all know that money a mickle makes a muckle,[8] but the box doesn't even have a mickle."

"Then we need more contributions from the likes of ourselves," replied Preston. "There is a heightened fear among the illiterate poor, assaulted on every corner by notices that they cannot understand. They see the word 'cholera' posted on each street; that's amplified the panic amongst the lower classes."

"But what's the point in cleaning?" said Deacon Johnston, sounding bemused. "Everybody knows the cause of this disease is a miasma from bad air, brought by the river filth, and as for doctors, some say

---

7   Parish pickaxe (19th cent) – a prominent nose.
8   Money a mickle makes a muckle (Scots proverb) – Many small amounts make a large amount.

the whole business is a plot to enable them to have more dead bodies for their research."

Young Ponsonby sneered. "Yes, I heard that too. Sounds like the devil's work, but the answer is in the Good Book." He held up his well-thumbed Bible. "The stories of Jonah, and Moses and Samson and Elijah are where the solution will lie."

"And how can we do business?" said Deacon Johnston. "My haberdashery shop will be ruined. You are aware I'm the chair of the Weavers' Corporation, and it's the same with the others: the Carters, Fleshers and Shoemakers. We are all in the same boat."

"The future is not ours to see, but I suggest that if you carry on with your trade, you will probably die," said Preston. "And you might take your children and wife with you."

"What do the doctors say?" said Commissioner White, turning to Preston.

Old Reverend McIntosh rose, indignation on his craggy features. "Forget the doctors and listen to what I say—and I know my colleagues in the upper courts of the Presbytery and the Church Synod agree."

His face reddened, irritation rising. Creaking, he stood up to reinforce his words.

"This pestilence is the creation of our Lord. Who to blame is as clear as day. Corinthians chapter six tells us…" He stood, voice rising with theatrical effect. "Neither fornicators, nor idolaters, nor adulterers, nor effeminate, nor abusers of themselves with mankind, nor thieves, nor coveters, nor drunkards, nor railers, nor extortioners…" He paused before shouting the final words: "…shall inherit the kingdom of heaven!"

"Hear hear!" exclaimed young Ponsonby.

"Humbug!" shouted Haddington. "It's all cholera humbug."

"It's that stench I can't stand," said Deacon Johnston. "It's foul, that smell of cholera. Sort of a fishy stink."

The deacon sniffed the air and then inhaled again.

"That aroma," he said, worry in his eyes. "It's in here."

"I'm sure it's coming from the bodies out in the churchyard," said Commissioner White.

For a moment, fifteen pairs of eyes darted back and forth. In unison, every black-clad man around the table now sniffed the air.

"No, it's most definitely in here. I'm sure of it," said Ponsonby.

"Meeting adjourned," cried the Reverend McIntosh.

Then, as one, all sixteen members of the Kirk Session rose and were surprisingly quick on their feet as they jostled and elbowed their way to the end of the hall and tried to cram themselves through the door at the same time.

32. Archie Woos Flossie
Saturday

Earnest Preston

William stepped through the entrance of the Stinking Pig and asked for Archie. The landlord nodded at the rickety stairs. When he reached the top, William startled to find Archie adding the finishing touches to the table, a tablecloth, napkins, silver cutlery, flowers and delicate crockery. He laughed out loud. "And wha are you trying to impress?"

"Wouldn't you like to ken, William, my boy? But none of your business. Concern yourself with your task. It's next Tuesday. You have the name, and delivery to be after dark, and same cottage as last time."

"So, what's with the fancy table? Have you got a—"

"Get oot and do your job," snapped Archie, yellow teeth bared.

With William gone, Archie returned downstairs and stepped outside. A fine evening, a hint of spring in the air.

A stroll round the corner to Vinegar Close. He was dressed in his finery, smart coat and a top hat. First date, important to create a favourable impression. For their next, he'd decided to take her to the cockfighting ring on the links. Was sure she'd enjoy it. Had also resolved to give her a peck on the cheek when they parted tonight. In future, he'd turn on the style so she saw the gentleman of means he was soon to be.

He'd daydreamed of it often since her husband was slain. Them living in a nice little house further upriver or along the coast. Somewhere away from the bustle, the two of them together, the sons moved on. Reckoned he now had sufficient influence to convince the Fraternity to use them in Edinburgh or somewhere else out the way, preferably in a different town. The daughter was a more awkward proposition. Flossie and she were very close, but hopefully that problem would also be sorted soon enough.

He knocked and Flossie opened the door.

"Flossie." Archie offered his widest smile. "As beautiful as you were fifteen years ago. You've not a wrinkle."

"Oh, Archie. Oh yes, I have." She giggled in that way Archie loved. "I often sit on it."

Archie laughed aloud.

He was glad she had made an effort. An almost new green dress with puffed sleeves reaching to the elbow from a dropped shoulder, and well-worn mid-length gloves. Even her hair was not the usual, parted at the centre and dressed in elaborate curls, loops and knots.

"William nicked the robe," she said, smiling. "Lark showed me how to do the hairstyle a while back."

"How is she?"

"Still weak but on the mend."

Flossie placed a linen cap trimmed with lace ribbon and frills and tied it under her chin, along with a matching green bonnet. She took his hand and stepped over the threshold.

In the courtyard at the bottom of the Cherry Tree House steps, the two elderly women gasped in surprise. Grannie O'Malley spluttered and spat. With Flossie on his arm, Archie strolled past and sneered.

"Oooh, whit a hussy," whispered Tin Pan Aggie.

A saunter round the corner and up the stairs of the Stinking Pig.

"Oh, Archie, it's lovely," said Flossie, admiring the table.

"A drink, madam?" He poured a glass of dark rum with an extravagant bow.

They sat. Archie gave a deep sigh and stared into her eyes. He was seldom so contented. It had been a long time since he had studied her so close. Hard to believe it was true, here with his beloved by his side at last. Was a marvel. The way the light caught her lovely hair... He visualised them couried up on a comfortable couch in front of a roaring fire, him putting his face between her breasts.

Small talk about her family first, her brood of offspring. Archie was surprised to hear that William and Lark were getting on well as Lark recuperated.

"He even brought her a gift," said Flossie. "Such a surprise, wouldn't have believed it possible a while back, were always at each other's throats. I suppose folk mellow as they grow older. Think William was more affected by his father's death than I kent at first."

"Oh aye," said Archie. "I'm sure deep doon he is a sensitive lad, despite the rough edges."

Archie braced himself, prepared to speak the words he had craved for so long.

"F… Fl… Flossie, I have something important to announce. For many years, I have fel—"

The door banged open and Mr Roberts came bustling in wearing an apron. Chops and cabbage steamed on two plates on his tray. Archie frowned.

"Oooh, smells lovely," said Flossie.

Mr Roberts fussed around, laying out the meat. He gave Archie a knowing look, which he ignored. Once he was gone, Archie lifted a chunk of pork to his mouth and chewed.

"Flossie, I have something I've wished to say to you for many years. I ha—"

"Tell me whit happened to Earnest."

He stopped, glanced up. Her expression was not the one he wanted. Archie almost gagged on his chop.

"E…Earnest? Well… whit… eh…"

"I want to understand. Explain whit transpired the day he died."

Was that a tear in her eye?

"When they killed him, you were present."

Archie sighed and peered at the cabbage and chops. His chest tightened, heavy with disappointment.

"Well…" He sat back in his chair and looked to the rafters. "How can I put it… I suppose Earnest was a showman to the end."

He dropped his eyes. "There were eight of them." His brow creased as he sought to recall the details. "Was a sizeable crowd above the beach, even a few stalls selling food and ale. I remember the whiff of fried pork. Already much drink taken, a day oot, a bit like the country fayre I suppose. Deans of guilds, lawyers, headmen of the corporations and societies, a few military in medals, a collection of the great and the good roped off in the spot offering the best view. Women in fine dresses with fellows with polished boots. The beach lined with hundreds of locals and a big mob doon fae Edinburgh."

Archie ran his fingers around the rim of his glass, memories flooding back.

"The pirates arrived in a donkey and cart. Withoot ceremony, they hanged their captain first, put him in the gibbet cage. The rest, left sitting on the sands in chains, waited for the tide to finish the job. 'Not enough rope,' shouted the magistrate."

Archie looked up. "Are you sure you want to hear this Flossie? Is it worth stirring up these auld memories? Earnest is long gone. It was years ago. You will only upset yourself."

"Aye," said Flossie. "Keeps coming back. I'm haunted by it. I should have been there, but I was too distraught. I want to understand whit happened."

Flossie's eyes were pleading. He cleared his throat.

"Most of the pirates were subdued. I remember the young laddie in the end was greetin' for his maw. Hanging might have been better. Quicker. As the tide came in, they struggled to stand when it splashed to their knees. Earnest tugged on his chain and walked forward, pulling towards the crowd far as he could, then just stood there looking at them. Some ladies squawked in alarm when he glared and smiled, a great big smile. Then he laughed—loud cackle, like a banshee. Had a mad look in his eyes."

Archie pushed his plate away and took his pipe and tobacco from his pocket.

"Your husband Abraham was on the beach, and Earnest picked him out. He pointed. I remember the words 'I hope you dinnae believe in ghosts, puffguts,' said in a growl like an animal. "Cause I'm coming for you.' There was a commotion when an older pirate couldn't take the chain's weight and went under the rising tide. As the water level rose to his neck, Earnest laughed his demented laugh and screamed, 'I'm coming for all of you.' No one responded; the magistrate just stood to the front looking smug, minister doing the usual praying for their souls and holding up his cross.

"Then," said Archie, noticing tears forming in Flossie's eyes. "Then the Firth covered him."

A surprise as the memory sent a shiver up his spine. He gasped. Was as if the air had altered, become heavier, as if moved. Disorientating.

Tears flowed down Flossie's cheeks. He looked away, filled his pipe, and lit up.

"Puffguts…" said Flossie. "But Abraham wasn't that fat. Why did Earnest call him puffguts?"

Archie shrugged. "As I say, he had the eyes of a madman, delirious. He didnae ken what he was saying."

Silence. Archie wondered whether it wise to fill that gap. He stalled. May not be the best time? But he couldn't help himself.

"D… did you ever see Earnest's box?"

"Whit box?"

"Wee, with a red mother-of-pearl dragon design. It contained something precious. We had agreed on a price and I had paid him a big deposit. Do you ken whitever happened to it?"

Flossie shook her head. "Not a clue whit you are talking aboot." She wiped away her tears. More silence.

"Nice chops," said Flossie.

33. Flossie Lives in Hope
Sunday

Flossie McColligan

Lark sat propped up, shrouded in the household's collection of blankets. Too unwell to attend the Floating Chapple. Other than for last night's disappointing date with Archie, Flossie rarely left her side. The smell of boiled bone broth wafted from the pot bubbling on the hearth.

Wee Eliza had been the first child Flossie had lost—a miracle Lark had not become the second. Though still weak, she was nevertheless improving. Yesterday, she'd had strength to rise and sit at the table. Able to feed herself as opposed to Flossie spooning into her mouth.

In the last few days, they'd had many visits from neighbours. Lark's survival was a marvel, best shared and celebrated. Flossie was grateful for the meagre donations of bread, dripping and coal from locals who couldn't afford it.

To Flossie's surprise, William continued to help. He'd previously brought Lark a gift of a bracelet and today brought home an onion, three carrots and potatoes, now added to the bone soup. Flossie was even more impressed when this afternoon he offered to accompany the younger children from the family upstairs to the now reopened Floating Chapple as no one else was well enough to take them. Flossie waved them off, a merry group with William at their head like the Pied Piper with Wee Andy and Eck to the rear.

"William seems to have changed, dinnae you agree?"

Lark managed a weak nod and croak.

"The past few days have shown he's a sensitive lad underneath," Flossie said. "Aren't boys funny that way? Sometimes they show their feelings in the strangest ways. Think wee Eliza's passing has affected him as much as it did us."

"Maybe," whispered Lark.

Flossie struggled to keep the emotion out of her voice. "He kens sickness can whisk away people you love in the blink of an eye, and it's taken him time getting over Abraham's murder. He missed his dad. It hit him far harder than I imagined, and took a long time coming to terms with it."

Lark offered a mirthless smile.

"You said it a while back, Maw. Men are men. Guess we will never understand them." Lark paused. "Have you seen any sign of Charlie Preston around the place since he took me to the doctor?"

Flossie turned away and stirred the broth. "No, not a peep. No word of him."

In fact, yesterday morning, Charlie Preston had approached Flossie on the Kirkgate at the market, as he had the day before, and also the day prior in St Andrew's Street. Agitated, he had blurted out a lot of nonsense about William trying to sell Lark. Flossie, of course, didn't believe him. The Prestons were always inclined to badmouth McColligans—sounded like the ravings of a madman. Flossie was wary of the young lad's deranged behaviour, especially now that William had turned the corner and he and Lark were getting along.

"That's a ridiculous thing to say," she had said firmly on each occasion before sending him on his way. "Pure badness, and I refuse to listen to any more of that talk. I'm thankful for what you did for Lark in taking her to see Dr Latta, but I won't hear any more of your stupid lies—now leave my family be."

***

At the Floating Chapple, the afternoon service had ended with a hymn. The Reverend Ponsonby led with his usual enthusiasm, sweating in shirtsleeves following his exertions. There was a buzz among the children as they anticipated the food to come. A long line snaked across the converted hulk, mouths watering as the ladies of the parish spooned potatoes and tripe topped with gravy into the wooden bowls.

Fat Archie slid in at the rear of the cavernous hold. In the commotion from the gaggle of excited youngsters, Ponsonby took Archie aside.

"I see this month's preference is absent today," he mumbled. "I hope there are not any difficulties with my order."

Archie tapped the side of his nose and grinned a yellow-toothed grin.

Ponsonby looked down his narrow beak, consternation in his voice. "I've already paid a handsome price."

"There's no problem," whispered Archie. "Tuesday evening, as agreed. We will deliver her on time."

On the other side of the hall, the McColligan boys took advantage as the line of youngsters became a melee around the large food tubs. With Big Zander, Deek and his brothers providing cover, William slipped behind the piano and rummaged through old Mrs Brown the pianist's coat. Three shillings. Next, a threadbare jacket hung on the chair. A few coppers and a very nice silk handkerchief, looked quality, similar to the one sold to Archie a while back.

At the rear of the hall, Charlie sat, despondent. No sign of Lark. She'd never missed the Chapple before, so why now? Was she still ill, or had she already been sold? At one point his glance met William's, but they just eyed each other and sneered. Nothing said.

34. Brotherly Love
Monday

Flossie McColligan

William popped his head round the door just after noon.

"Got you this nice bit of meat, will help strengthen you."

He dropped it on the table. From Lark, a weak smile. She lay on the blankets, chalk white, her recovery slow.

"I hope she keeps this doon, might build up her energy," said William.

Flossie was surprised, unsure of how to react, not altogether believing. "And where did the money for that appear fae?"

William winked. "Remember, I'm working at the timber yard two days a week. So bought with my wages."

Well, miracles can happen, thought Flossie. *Wonder where he nicked it.*

She knew he was lying, but was thrilled, struggling to stop a smile forming on her generous lips. Maybe things were looking up.

A William transformed. He had always been a troublesome boy. Abraham had beaten him often, but that never seemed to change his wild behaviour. Flossie had noted his genuine upset at wee Eliza's death; now it appeared he'd had an awakening and a soft spot after all. All that bravado and bluster gone. The scare with Lark had upset him, that was obvious, but in a good way.

Well, that's a gracious gesture, thought Flossie.

Lark sat up. "Thanks, William. I'll eat it tonight."

William turned. "Hey, sister, I'd do anything to help you get better. And good news that a pal of mine, works in a big apothecary up in the toon, has offered me some of this amazing tonic. Can perform marvels. It's not a cure, but helps you regain your energy after the cholera. I should get it tomorrow."

He bounded out the door. Lark was still wobbly when standing. She returned to her bed with a hungry look at the slab of meat. Flossie prayed she'd be able to keep it down.

"Well, isn't that wonderful," said Flossie. "What a nice brother you have."

***

In Giles Street, Charlie paced back and forward like a caged animal, desperate. Tried entering Vinegar Close more than once, but William's crew now guarded both ends. Wracked his brains about discovering another way to get a message to Lark and warn her of William's plan. He wished they could read and write properly; would have sent a note.

That morning, he again sought out Flossie, this time in Old Flesh Market. He'd tried talking to her repeatedly, but this time she just showed anger, refused to speak and pushed past him.

"It's true, I swear," he pleaded, grabbing her arm. "William is going to sell her—he telt me that himself."

Flossie turned and looked him hard in the eye. "Now, for the last time, I'm aware you helped take her to Doctor Latta, and I am grateful. But if you imagine you can come daily and repeat terrible things aboot my son, well, I'm not prepared to listen. William may not be perfect, but he would never do that. Sell his own sister, dinnae be ridiculous. Are you mad?"

She turned. "As it so happens, he has been showering gifts on her of late. Now get awa, you stupid boy, and don't come bothering my family again." Flossie stomped off along towards Tollbooth Wynd.

Charlie hung his head. How to save Lark? When was William going to sell her? How much time did he have left?

Clearly there was only one way, the direct route, and that needed reinforcements.

35. An Unwelcome Surprise
Tuesday

Lark McColligan

Lark, knees shaky, stood by the hearth. Flossie had rustled up more vegetable broth, and last night, the meat William had supplied was the first solid thing Lark had been able to keep down. So juicy, after managing a few mouthfuls, her appetite returning.

The temperature had risen, the days of heavy rain ended and a few rays of evening sun found their way through the close into corners it had not seen for months. Lark's strength was much improved; she managed to step outside and join the chat on the steps of Cherry Tree House. The latest rumour was that the pandemic had passed its peak.

"Will you be well enough tae go cigar hunting tomorrow, now you're cured?" said Grannie O'Malley. "Hope so, cos I've not had a smoke for days. Cannae wait for that sweet smell in ma pipe."

"Wis your own fault you caught cholera in the first place," said Tin Pan Aggie. "You must have been eating too much cold fruit. That can cause it, ya ken, or maybe because you have been too emotional with all these laddies skulking aboot, droolin' after you."

"Have your bowels been regular?" said Grannie.

"Did the quack bleed you?" said Aggie.

Lark shook her head.

"Mind you, there's been a heavy harr on mornings of late, might have been that caused it," said Aggie.

Lark couldn't find the energy or will to answer.

"Anyway, it's a miracle you're saved. Must be because we prayed for you—didn't we, Aggie?"

"Oh, aye, we did, every day."

William appeared out the stair, grabbed Lark's hand and gently pulled her away.

"After so many days in bed, a gentle walk will do you good, to take the air," he said. "It's whit the doctor recommended."

"Aye, your brother is right for once," said Grannie.

"Let's get these legs moving."

Lark took William's arm, and they shuffled out the courtyard.

"Sounds to me she has escaped fae the devil's clutches," said Grannie.

"Saved by one o' they evil doctors," said Tin Pan Aggie with a scowl. "Huh, so more like she was in league with the devil, if you ask me."

Grannie O'Malley nodded, hacked and spat. "Aye, nae doubt you're right, Aggie."

William and Lark strolled up the close into Giles Street, in the fading light. They turned towards the river.

"Can we wipe the slate clean?" said William. "I realise we've not seen eye to eye in the past, but you're my sister, and after wee Eliza, I dinnae want to lose you as well."

"You're not the easiest to live with, William. You need to get Big Zander off my back for a start."

"I will, I'm sorry. I just become angry sometimes, with whit happened to Father and then wee Eliza, it's been eating away at me, didnae understand how to cope with it. I ken I have to change my ways."

Lark considered whether to mention Charlie Preston, but decided against it. Best not antagonise William when it looked like relations were improving.

"We have had oor differences of late, Lark, but now, I just want you healthy."

They reached the corner with Cable's Wynd, then down the vennel, through the soapworks. A harr rolled in, the chill from the sea merging with the day's smoke and soot as the sun fell below the horizon.

"Let's go home," said Lark. "We've walked far enough; it's getting dark."

They turned.

"Oh," said William. "And I got you that tonic fae my pal." He removed a small bottle from his jacket. "It's guaranteed to increase your energy. Was so lucky to get it, normally costs a fortune."

Lark unstopped the little flask and sipped. "Tastes funny."

"Drink it all," said William. "It will do you the world of good."

Lark emptied its contents into her mouth, then decided she had to mention Charlie. They needed to sort it out.

From Sheriff Brae, they turned up Sheephead Wynd back towards home.

"We need to talk aboot Charlie Preston," said Lark. "He saved my life." She stumbled. William caught her arm. "I'm still no right, feel a bit woozy. Need to take it easy for a bit."

At the top of the Wynd, Lark gave a brief squeal. Her body swayed to the side, balance going, saw double. Lifted her hand and grabbed William's shoulder. The last thing she saw was his wide smile before everything drifted away.

***

William caught her as she slumped, pulled her into a doorway, put his fingers to his mouth and whistled. Zander appeared round the corner carrying a jute sack. They spoke no words as they pushed Lark's feet into the bag.

"Best tie her," said Zander. "In case she wakes up."

William rustled in his pockets and plucked out the handkerchief he had taken from the jacket at the Floating Chapple. He passed it to Zander, who tied her hands. They pulled the sack up over her head and knotted the string.

Soon afterwards, the road upriver dark and quiet, Zander helped lift Lark onto William's back before a final check the coast was clear. William moved off silently, his sister's unconscious body slung over his shoulder, keeping to the shadows cast by the half-moon as a harr thickened. He slipped out of town via Sherriff Brae.

36. The Key
Wednesday

Lark McColligan

Lark roused, head fuzzy, the scratch of sackcloth on her face, fibres up her nose. Darkness. She tried moving her hands, tied in front. Panic as she tugged. She forced herself to slow her breath. Where was she? A smell of mildew and dust.

She quietened her breathing and listened hard. Footsteps, thumps coming from the next room.

"Who's there?"

What had happened? Was like a dream—William's smiling face, but then what?

"Ah."

A voice she recognised. A stab of terror through her heart.

"You have awakened, my dear. I've been lingering all day. Looks like they gave you a modest overdose, but now, at last, we can have our little party."

An overdose? Her face was taut with shock. Who? She tried to remember. The seeing double, that wee bottle—or was that just her imagination?

She felt the sack now pulled, then lugged along the ground. A bump on her knee as she felt herself drawn through a doorway.

"But first I'll block the entrance, in case you decide to leave early."

Lark gritted her teeth, fighting the fear.

"Whit are you doing? Let me go." Her mouth filled with sack fibres when she spoke.

The sound of dragging furniture. The sack was untied before being pulled from the bottom, sending her tumbling full length onto the floor. She blinked, shook her head, struggled to take in her surroundings.

A room with an enormous bed, a shadow crossing the wall. She twisted round and gasped at the sight of a naked Reverend Ponsonby lighting an oil lamp, the shabby space suddenly bright. He spun and smiled at her through crooked teeth. With one hand, he picked up leather straps from the chest of drawers, with the other a large hunting knife.

"Now, my dear, don't be afraid. If you come and lay on the bed, we can get you secured. It's what the Lord has demanded."

Lark stood, pushing herself against the wall, struggling, legs shaking, awkward with tied hands.

"Go fuck yourself."

Ponsonby's expression hardened. "Oh, Miss McColligan, that's not the spirit." He advanced towards her. "It's much more fun if you take part in our modest ceremony, a marriage in the eyes of our Lord."

The reverend rushed forwards, blade high. Lark sprang into the air, and in one fluid movement rolled onto and over the bed. She caught a whiff of Ponsonby's foul breath as he lunged. The steel slashed a tear in her ragged dress.

"Oooh, playing hard to get." On his thin mouth, a devilish smile.

He stepped around the bed, eyes sharp with that familiar expression of a man on a mission. He pointed the knife at her. Lark squirmed, cornered. Glanced at his groin; the reverend was becoming excited. Lark leaped over the bed, but Ponsonby grabbed her foot. He lunged and forced himself upon her. She thrashed beneath, trying to squirm away, but he was too heavy, too determined.

"You have such a tiny little cock," she hissed. Baring her teeth, she bit his ear and yanked with all her strength.

"Owww!" Ponsonby threw himself backwards and drew away, holding his bloodied ear, face reddened, temper rising. He raised the knife.

"Well, may be true, but that won't save a trollop like you."

The reverend moved a pace towards her. Despite her panic, with nothing to lose, she slid from the bed and took a step forward. A flash of surprise in Ponsonby's eyes as Lark rose on the toes of her right foot and her left foot arced skyward, a swift sharp kick connecting with his balls, a sickening squish. The reverend swung the knife as he doubled over in agony, crying out. Lark swerved before skipping over the bed once again.

"Aargh, you little bitch! You'll pay for that," he said, clutching himself, desperate eyes on her. She saw rage and madness there, dagger in hand, face beetroot red.

Lark fell against the wall, a painful poke in her back, looked round. With awkward hands, she removed the rusty key from the cupboard, stepped inside, placed the key in the lock, pulled the door and twisted. A click as the reverend hobbled over with an enraged shout, thrusting the point of his blade into the wood.

"Aargh! Come out, you vile little hoor, come out at once!"

Lark cowered and pushed herself against the rear of the closet.

"Come out!" he screamed.

Then she heard Ponsonby muttering to himself, a stomp of footsteps out the room that quickly returned. A deafening clang as something big hit the door, then again, and once more, but it held, the cupboard raining dust with each impact. The sound of heavy panting and cursing under his breath, then quiet. Long seconds passed.

The door thumped again.

"Open the bloody door."

Bang.

"The Lord God said, is not good that man should be alone, I will make him a helper fit for him."

Bang.

"Open it!"

Bang.

"Fuck off!" roared Lark.

Ponsonby's voice rose to a howl. "The book of Timothy says let a woman learn with all submissiveness. Do not permit women to exercise authority over a man; she is to remain quiet."

Bang.

"So, my dear, you will do as the Bible commands."

There was desperation in his tone. Bang.

"Open it, you little bitch!"

Bang.

Voice louder. "Or I'll kill you! I'll kill you!"

Then a thud as she sensed his body slump away. The creak of springs, he was sitting on the bed, breathing heavy after his exertions.

"You can't stay in there forever, girl, and I'm in no hurry. Am prepared to wait."

Lark stayed silent and shivered. Time passed, nothing said.

A sound.

First, a tiny squeak like air being released from a bladder, a low groan. It stopped. Then a sob, louder, the hint of an unusual stink. Cupboard dust? Or something else?

Lark removed the key from the lock, crouched to the keyhole. There was little to see in the gloom other than the soft light cast from the lamp. Moving shadows, the air thick. Was there a vapour?

The moan, now a shout.

"No! Nooo!" The reverend's cry.

Was that a second voice? But how? She would have heard anyone entering. Someone laughing? No? Was there another?

She held the key tight in her hand, fear overwhelming her curiosity. Then a piercing wail, Ponsonby's voice, high-pitched. "Oh Lord, save me."

Another mind-numbing shriek.

"Devil!"

The sound of desperate gasps, like a lamb she once saw strangled by a butcher at market. The thump of a heavy weight hitting the other side of the door, followed by a scraping, a slithering and a thud.

Then nothing. She looked through the keyhole again. Darkness and silence. She listened. Minutes passed. No breathing, no sound. Was it a trick?

Lark dropped to her knees, made herself as comfortable as possible, and waited, until she fell into a fitful sleep.

37. Angus Digs Deeper
Thursday

Superintendent Andrew Angus

Lark shook herself awake, cramped. Every bone ached. Her stomach growled with hunger. Hands tied, she rubbed her eyes. Took a moment to remember where she was, put an ear to the door and listened. She squinted through the keyhole. Daylight, silence. Was he waiting to pounce? And the noises at night, the strange cries… She could make no sense of it. Was it a dream?

Muffled banging, men's voices in the distance. More thumps.

"Reverend Ponsonby!" A shout.

A loud thud, wood snapping, the scrape of furniture moving next door.

"It's the police. Superintendent Angus and Constable Ross."

A crack of something breaking, the thump of footsteps in the room.

With her hands still knotted, Lark slipped the key in the lock. It opened with a click. Two uniforms stooped over Ponsonby's naked skinny body. His face was contorted in a grotesque expression, eyes wide. The policemen spun round together, open-mouthed.

With a creak, the door swung open. Lark held her tied palms in front of her, smiled an embarrassed smile.

"Well, well," said Angus. "What have we here?"

He looked down at Ponsonby's body and back to Lark then shook his head. "You look like you have seen a ghost, lassie."

Angus turned. "Constable Ross, can you pop down to Dr Latta's dispensary? Tell him I've got a body I want him to examine."

Lark held out her bound hands. "Eh, could you?"

***

Two hours later, she was home. Flossie, eyes puffy but smiling, sat in the good chair, Lark on the stool. Superintended Angus paced the room.

"We had heard a few rumours about Reverend Ponsonby, so I suppose you providing evidence they were true is very convenient, has tidied up the mystery of the vanishing urchins."

"And they kidnapped my daughter," said Flossie, anger in her eyes. "So, whit are you going to do aboot it?"

"Pah," said Angus. He pulled out and held up the handkerchief that had bound Lark's hands. "What I'm interested in is this hankie." He turned to Lark. "Yet you tell me you were already secured with this when you woke in the sack."

"Aye," said Lark. "It's true, I swear."

"But what aboot the kidnapping?" said Flossie, bristling.

"Then it can't be Ponsonby who took you, so who tied you? And where did they get this handkerchief?"

"So, the Leith police dismisseth us," said Flossie, scorn in her voice.

"That's correct," said Lark. "I remember I woke up in a sack and someone had bound my wrists before Ponsonby dumped me oot."

"Whoever tied you?" said Angus. "That's the information I need."

"I dinnae ken. All I can recall is seeing double before I passed out. Must have been weak from the cholera."

"And a fellow is dead," said Flossie. "A churchman, no less. Wha would believe it?"

"Mores to the point, where did the handkerchief come from?" mused Angus. "It doesn't add up, too many variables. I've had Dr Latta go to the cottage to examine Ponsonby's body. His theory's that it's most likely poisonous fumes from the river that killed him. There was a heavy fog last night. He tells me the paper mills often use so much chlorine it can become dangerously concentrated under certain conditions." He turned to Lark. "So, your story of hearing someone else in the room can't be true. You were scared out of your wits, so you must have dreamt it, lassie. And anyway, the door was barred from the inside when we broke it down, so it's impossible."

Lark shrugged. Angus continued to pace and fret.

"And where is your brother, William? And he gave you that tonic? Is he mixed up in this?"

He turned to Flossie. "Put water to boil, woman. I want to go over it again. We are going nowhere until I sort this out."

***

From the Yardheads, Tommy, Charlie, Sam and Henry turned into Vinegar Close. Moving fast, it was too easy. They rushed Big Zander before he raised the alarm. Charlie jumped on his back, Tommy booted him in the balls, Henry smashed a piece of coal into his mouth before together they pushed him into a coal shed and barred the entrance. The handful of other younger guards scattered as the Prestons charged into Lark's courtyard.

Charlie turned to his brothers. "I can take it from here."

He thumped the McColligans' door. Flossie answered. Charlie flustered.

"Lark. I need to speak to Lark."

He pushed past into the single room and sank to his knees, shivered with relief. Lark, looking pale, was by the fire.

"I've been trying to see you for days," he panted. "To warn you. William's intention is to seize and sell you."

"You better take a seat, lad," said Superintendent Angus, popping his head from behind the door. "And tell me everything."

Charlie blurted out his story. His fight with William and what he'd said, how he'd tried to forewarn Lark but William's crew had kept him away.

Superintendent Angus held out the hanky. "They tied the lassie with this. I learned it was stolen from Mr Preston, the banker, but I spotted Ponsonby with it in Archie McTavish's shop." He turned to Lark, frowning. "The mystery, young lady, is if they bound you before arriving at Ponsonby's, then where had this handkerchief been? Who had it?"

"It has to be William!" cried Charlie.

"Naw," whimpered Flossie. "Never."

Angus rubbed his jaw. "If your brother was the one who kidnapped you, as this lad says, then how did he get it, other than Ponsonby must have given him it. But I know they stole it first from Preston, the banker."

"But what about the kidnapping?" said Flossie, indignant. "Surely that's more important than a handkerchief."

"Kidnapping." Angus looked down his nose. "We really have no concern with your petty household squabbles. What interests me is those who rob lead citizens of the town. The simple fact is, the next commissioner and new provost will not tolerate it. We won't have it, no argument, and more than my job's worth. You and the rest of the rabble can kill each other for what I care, just as your husband and"—he pointed at Charlie—"his father did." He stroked his whiskers and mused, "Though I suspect that pair of vagabonds probably did us all a favour."

"That little bastard. I cannae believe it's true," growled Flossie, grappling with the emotions running through her mind. Her earlier relief now become anger.

Angus rubbed his jaw a second time. "Though I would like a word with young William." He turned to Lark and Flossie. "Where is he?"

Lark felt weak. So much had happened that day and it wasn't even noon. The policeman held up the hankie.

"So, let's go over it again, the initials AP, the girl's hands tied before she arrived there. I need to find out by whom, if it's not Ponsonby."

Flossie sobbed. "Can't believe it true, William selling his own flesh and blood."

A rumble and thump. The door burst open.

"Right, Maw, where's my dinner? I'm starv…"

William stood slack-jawed, struggling to comprehend that Charlie Preston was sitting in his house in front of him with his mother and sister. He glanced at Flossie.

On her face was a deep frown. "William."

He peered at Lark, on her brow a deeper frown.

"Oh, brother, so you have changed your ways, have you?"

Angus's firm hand clamped down on William's shoulder.

"Ha, William, my boy. I've a few questions."

Angus grabbed William's lapels and swung him against the wall.

"Whit?" yelled William. "I've no done anything. Whit's going on?"

In one fluid movement, Superintendent Angus slipped out his truncheon, then gave a sharp flick on William's head with a hollow-sounding pop. William screamed and fell to the floor. Lark, Flossie and Charlie juddered in shock.

"Now," said Angus, peering down with an insincere smile. "Let's examine the facts."

He pointed at Charlie. "One: this lad says you sought to sell your sister, and I think he is speaking the truth, as we discovered her tied up in Reverend Ponsonby's cupboard."

Angus held up a pair of fingers. "Two: the kidnapper secured Lark with this handkerchief before they delivered her to the Reverend Ponsonby's cottage."

He held up three. "Three: this hanky belonged to Mr Preston, the banker. In the statement that gentleman provided following he and the good Dr Latta's assault and robbery in the street, you fit the description of one of his assailants."

Four fingers raised. "Four: I saw the Reverend Ponsonby buying this very same hanky in Archie McTavish's scrap shop. So, one mystery is, how did it arrive at Archie's place? And I presume the answer is that you sold it following your assault and theft from Mr Preston."

"Naw," cried William. "I didn—"

Angus took a step back and gave William a sharp kick to the ribs.

"And the second riddle is: how did it end up round your sister's wrists? Though I suspect that is because Ponsonby gave it to you for that very purpose."

"Naw, naw," squealed William. "I found it on the street. It was Zander McFarlane wha tied it."

"Ha." Angus chuckled. "An admission of Big Zander's guilt if ever there was one, which we can now add to your own. When put together with Mr Preston's assault and robbery then, whichever way you look at it, young William, you're nicked."

"Naw, naw!" screamed William, trying to rise. Angus kicked him in the stomach, before grabbing him by the hair, pulling him to his feet and throwing him onto the bench.

"However, there is still one unanswered question." Angus bent forward until their eyes were level. "Who you are working for."

William rubbed his skull and groaned.

"I… eh… dinnae ken nothing."

Flossie lunged and aimed a slap at his head. "Tell him!" she screamed.

"Wouldn't be a fat man, by any chance?" snapped the superintendent.

William looked up, defeat in his eyes. Angus raised his baton.

"Naw," squealed William, cowering.

"So tell me his name."

"Eh, eh, it was Archie, Archie McTavish. I kidnapped lassies to order for his customers."

"Ah, well, thank you for that, my boy," said Angus with a satisfied smirk. He pulled out his notebook and scribbled.

"Now." He tapped his teeth with his pencil before returning it to his breast pocket "The next piece of information I need…" He raised his truncheon again. "Who does Archie McTavish work for?"

"I dinnae ken," said William, pleading.

"Then enough," said Angus. "Constable Ross, cuff him and get down the station. Let's see if we can beat it out of you, in advance of you going before the sheriff on Saturday."

"I've no idea," screamed William, anguish on his face. "He tells me nothing, I only do as I'm telt."

Constable Ross stood him up, yanked back his arms, snapped on the handcuffs and hauled him towards the door.

"And, Constable, once you have locked him up, see if you can find McTavish and bring him in for a chat."

Superintendent Angus gave a satisfied snort and made to leave.

"Well, the good news is that we sorted out Ponsonby and the missing youngsters. Who would have thought it, eh, a man of the Lord? I suppose it goes to show that it takes all sorts. And, now I sense we are getting closer to the killer of my informants, and to discovering who is behind all the crime, we need to bring in Archie. I think he's had his fingers in more pies than just selling the urchins."

He nodded and followed Constable Ross, who dragged William out the door.

"Well," said Tin Pan Aggie as the officer huckled William across the courtyard. The two old women shuffled back to their usual spot on the steps, away from the McColligans' window.

"Did you listen to all that?" said Grannie. "Wha would have believed it? Ah telt you all along it wasn't the gypsies."

"Ah cannae believe it, I'm speechless," said Tin Pan Aggie.

"Aye, well, that's a first." Grannie lowered herself on the steps of Cherry Tree House, took out her pipe, hacked, and spat.

Back in the McColligans' house, Charlie, Flossie and Lark sat in stunned silence.

Flossie, her face white, gave a long sigh. "Whit's next, I wonder?"

Charlie stood and pulled Lark to her feet. They hugged, they kissed.

Flossie sighed, and then a fatigued laugh. "Well, in for a penny, in for a pound. Think we have had enough excitement for yin day, but given I now see what you pair have been up to these past few weeks, there's yin thing you ought to ken."

Lark and Charlie turned. "Whit?" they asked together.

"You two are cousins," said Flossie.

"Eh?" said Lark, bewilderment in her eyes.

"I never finished telling you that story of the pirate's execution."

"The pirates? What pirates?" said Charlie.

Lark took his hand, sat him on the bench and explained the details of Earnest's death.

Flossie took a deep breath. "You see, Lark, unlike your three brothers, your father's not the drunken Abraham. Your father was Earnest, Earnest Preston."

"The pirate who died," said Lark, confusion on her face.

"Aye, once we resumed our relationship, I became pregnant to him with you, though I wasn't aware of that at the time he was executed. I should have telt you while ago now—Earnest had finished with my wee sister, and I'd had enough of Abraham, so we got together in secret, were going to run off, take William with us and move to a new toon to start again. But the day before we were due to steal awa, they arrested him, and I never saw him from that day on. Broke my heart."

Lark stood open mouthed, reeling from this knowledge, struggling to let it sink in.

They sat in silence. A full forty-five seconds passed.

"Can you marry your cousin?" said Lark.

Charlie gasped, pure joy.

"Dinnae have a clue," said Flossie. "We will have to go to the Kirk and ask the minister."

38. Archie Takes a Telling
Friday

Archie McTavish

The coach swayed on its springs as Archie's substantial frame stepped onto wet cobbles. The fatigued horses stamped their feet before the coach trundled onward. A damp night, heavy rain earlier, gloomy but for the glow of the new gaslights along the Shore. A gusty blast from the west, clearing the usual stink of river and whale sheds. Archie was in fine spirits and sported a brand-new top hat.

Yesterday had been spent dealing with a profitable bit of business up town for Fraternity colleagues. He'd visited a few of the capital's better shops, spent the extra income now flowing his way. The only downside of the new arrangement was that in future he'd have to guard against envious enemies and grasping friends. He headed straight for Flossie's, pushing through the crowds gathered around the gangplank of the *Walter Scott*, the London and Edinburgh Steam Packet Company's sleek ship.

The noise of its two throbbing engines drowned the shouts of porters as they hoisted cases and crates on board, large and small. Billowing steam swirled across the wharf. The first-class passengers had already embarked, making their way to the fine state rooms on the upper deck, their apartments glittering with flickering lanterns. Archie pushed through the throng of lower-class patrons, gift in hand: a hatbox with a new bonnet. The stage set to make his move. Their initial date hadn't been the success he'd hoped, though he expected she would need a sympathetic ear now with her daughter gone. Time to draw her in.

He slipped through the lane to Tollbooth Wynd, then up Old Fleshmarket towards the Yardheads and into Vinegar Close, where he knocked on the McColligans' door under the courtyard's single whale-oil light.

"Archie." Surprise on her face, Flossie blew out her cheeks and took a step back. "Lark is home."

Archie's brow furrowed, struggled to disguise his astonishment.

"So," said Flossie, lifting her chin and pursing her lips.

Archie, eyes down, scratched his ear and shuffled his feet. "I bought you this present," he said, holding out the hatbox and looking into her lovely eyes.

Flossie gave a hard stare, ignored the package.

"The truth's etched on your face, Archie, and William's in jail. He has told the polis that you were behind it."

"Eh… eh…" stuttered Archie, dismay on his face.

Flossie's chin jutted. Those vivid hazel eyes Archie so admired burned like fire under the lamplight. They bore into him.

"You… you nasty, nasty man."

"But… I… we… em…"

Flossie stepped forward, and with a sharp right hook, hit him hard across the jaw. He flinched.

"And do you ken whit else I've been thinking, now I've learned whit you are capable of?"

Archie put his hand to his face, stunned "Whit was that for, woman?"

"When Earnest pointed at Abraham before they executed him, where were you standing?"

"Eh… eh… mmm… eh…" Archie mumbled. "Cannae recall."

"You're a liar," snapped Flossie. "And withoot that unkempt beard, you would be a bare-faced liar."

"B-but, Flossie…"

"It wasn't Abraham McColligan he was pointing at, was it? It was you, you and you alone who telt the magistrates where Earnest made his money. You had discovered the truth, hadn't you? Well, your crime was as bad as his."

Archie's body lurched with her words. His face drooped, bushy brows narrowed, his world crumbling.

"Puffguts!" she shouted.

"Awa with you, woman. You're making no sense."

Archie looked away, but recoiled. She had hit her mark. Flossie's expression grew more savage.

"You." She stabbed him hard in the chest with her finger, and then again with each word. "You're a scoundrel, a liar, a hornswoggler[9]."

---

9   *Hornswoggler (19th cent) – cheat/fraudster.*

"B-but, Flossie, there must have been a misunderstanding. I got you this gift." He held up the hatbox again.

Flossie pushed it away. Voice rising, she stepped towards him, forcing retreat. "And whit was all that aboot Earnest's box? Explain!"

He stumbled backwards at the ferocity of her attack.

"I… It was a jewel. He needed cash, I was going to buy it, I paid Earnest a deposit but I never received the thing, he was in jail before I could get it."

"You're an excuse for a human being." She moved an inch from his face. "A gibface. You're nothing but a fat, slimy bastard."

She grabbed him by the lapels and pushed hard.

"And as for Lark and your filthy wee schemes…"

Archie made to bat her away. "Look, I dinnae ken what you are talking aboot, Flossie. You've got it all wrong."

She swung at him with her left, Archie ducked.

"You're a coward."

"But, Flossie, please, dinnae you understand? I did it for us."

Flossie stopped and stood to her full height, wide eyed, gasping with quivering lips. She blew out her cheeks. Flushed face, throbbing veins, clenched jaw. She bared her teeth.

"Do you think I would ever let a limp-cocked flapdoodle[10] like you anywhere near me, with your grotesque belly and your fat malmsey nose[11]?"

Archie retreated, and turned away.

"Ach. To hell with you, woman."

Flossie pushed him hard in the back, again with both hands. He stumbled over a broken brick and his new hat fell off and rolled into the sour midden fed by the leaking cesspit in the courtyard's corner. He bent to retrieve it. Flossie, eyes blazing, gave her fiercest scowl and kicked his backside full force as he tried to rise from the stink. Archie tottered and stumbled forwards, slipping on the sludge and falling full-length into the midden.

"Aye, that's right, Archie. That's where you belong, so awa you and lie in your own pish."

With that, Flossie turned and strode back to her stair, the door slamming behind her.

---

10   *Flapdoodle (19th cent) – sexually incompetent.*

11   *Malmsy nose (19th cent) – heavily acned nose (from too much malmsey wine).*

Archie stood. Struggling to believe what had just happened, he shook off the filth, lifted his hat and hobbled towards the courtyard entrance.

"Och," said Tin Pan Aggie as he passed. "The path of true love never runs smooth."

Archie gave a low growl in the women's direction before walking forlornly out the yard and headed for the Stinking Pig.

Grannie O'Malley hacked, spat, then nodded as she watched him leave. "Aye, never a truer word spoken, Aggie, though never understood whit she saw in him anyways."

Archie stumbled into the street. *How did it all go so wrong?* Plans in tatters, mind racing. His heart thumped under his coat, tearing with regret and longing. His beloved Flossie had spurned him. William McColligan had been arrested, so Superintendent Angus would be on his tail, and if caught, he may end up shackled next to some stinking reprobate in a line for transportation. And worst of all, likely a visit from his gang masters in the Fraternity of Unholy Blood, very soon and no doubt up a dark alley with a knife. The only option was to take a barge and make a run for it. He needed to pick up his stash of money.

Archie bought a bottle of best whisky at the Stinking Pig before heading straight for his shop, panic in his step as he hastened along the Shore. Flossie was lost to him. He couldn't face it. Stopped to glance behind, uneasy. Emotions were to be feared; they only caused pain. William would cry like a baby now the superintendent had him in custody; Archie didn't have long. The rain was now heavier, dark, the quay and Broad Wynd quiet, only a murmur coming from the taverns with their dim lights. God, he needed a drink.

An hour later, just before midnight, with Bluebell at his heels, Archie held himself against the doorframe and fumbled with his keys. A half-moon gave enough light for him to lock the shop door on the third attempt. He gripped the keys hard until he pushed them back into his pocket. He pulled the near-empty whisky bottle out of another and swigged before replacing it. He staggered down the lane towards the Shore. An icy blast of wind tunnelled up Broad Wynd, fast clouds scudding above, visible in the moonlight. He tugged his frock coat tighter around his neck. A scuffle of feet behind him as three urchins squeezed themselves into the alcove at his shop, and a rustle as they covered themselves with an old, torn piece of canvas.

Archie turned and cursed them once before swaying down the street. He almost tripped over Bluebell as he stepped onto the Shore. Lurched forward, only preventing a fall by grabbing the top of a barrel outside the ship chandler's. Wind and rain swirling, he stumbled across the cobbles until he stood on the edge of the wharf, staring into the dark mass of the river as it sped towards the sea, fast and high, swollen with last night's deluge.

Feeling the tears rising, belly lurching, he held a breath, attempting to stop them, but then they came. He sobbed hard, soon a flood. He couldn't understand how he was so misunderstood; could Flossie not realise he just believed they might start again, the two of them? Now drained, overwhelmed, he turned and scanned the buildings that lined the quayside. Shuttered, inhabitants asleep, lonely, not a single light.

He screamed at the top of his voice, "I only wanted to be loved!"

Archie breathed hard. The wind abruptly dropped and the rain suddenly stopped. The air seemed heavier, then heavier again. He glanced around. Deserted. An eerie silence, no sound other than the churning river. A smell he didn't recognise, not the usual sewage and rotting fish. What was it? Oil? Some kind of broken sewer? No, more a vapour. Or a mist.

Was that a dim light in front of him? Or an apparition. He blinked and tried to focus. Was it on the other side? The crash of the fast-flowing water was now louder. A sudden tension in his neck, a crushing of his temples, banging and rushing in his eardrums. Another sound, he recognised it, he was sure he had heard it before. He leaned forward holding his gut, and vomited. Whisky or fear? A distant laugh, like a cackle, but inside his head.

Archie felt unnerved, disorientated, looked left and right. Nothing. Someone was watching him, laughing at him. He drew the bottle from his pocket and sucked out the last drops, swung hard and threw the empty as far as he could across the maelstrom. The action made him dizzy. A sharp, sudden blast and a blade of chill wind on his back as if pushed. He started to drift, his balance, the axis, his reference point gone.

Only Bluebell saw him fall, or heard the splash. She whined, sniffed the air, then turned and howled at the moon.

39. Justice
Saturday

Flossie McColligan

Flossie had decided to attend the trial, but when she saw the queue she thought maybe not to bother and go to the market instead. It stretched halfway down Constitution Street, the usual array of spectators for the Saturday courts by the Town Hall, grumbling in the drizzle. Hopeful housewives, old men with grim faces, apprehensive young women holding back tears with babes in arms, whole families who were regulars, a gaggle of their whinging children in tow. Then, feeling a stab of guilt, Flossie changed her mind and joined the line.

She noted Superintendent Angus arriving on foot, boots freshly blackened, his dress tunic brushed, badges polished and fob watch pinned with care. Looked like he'd taken time over shaving and oiling his hair. He pushed aside a family of tinkers at the front of the queue and nodded to the dour constables on the door before entering the austere court chambers.

Soon, Flossie made her way into the packed room and pushed her way to the front of the public gallery.

"All rise for the Sheriff."

The crowded courtroom stood as the ermine robe of Lord Haddington mounted the steps. He winced, and sat tentatively before nodding to his officials.

"Bring the first case."

Then followed the familiar array of bread thieves, wife beaters, swindlers, vagrants, debtors, trespassers, forgers, charlatans and ladies of the night. Haddington passed sentences with a tap of his gavel, rarely looking up from a volume he was enjoying hidden under his papers, the last in the series of Walter Scott's *Waverley* novels.

With limited funds, most offenders were dependent on the court lawyer to defend them. Hercules Timpkins, a spotty young man in an ill-fitting suit who, Flossie noted, appeared to tremble each time he was compelled to speak. There was little in the way of leniency. Groans came from the crowd as friends and relatives were led away, harsh penalties of a fine, birching or imprisonment.

The final case of the day, William McColligan and Alexander McFarlane, were dragged from the cells in handcuffs.

"Superintendent Angus, your statement," called Lord Haddington.

Angus rose and held up the handkerchief for all to see. His distinct voice told the story of its theft from the banker, Mr Alexander Preston, and subsequent discovery in the home of Reverend Ponsonby via the shop of Archie McTavish. He spoke of the tireless endeavours made in tracking down these two criminals and how police skill and daring had been rewarded by the making of arrests, solving the riddle of vanishing urchins and the unravelling of criminal networks. He then told of a possible connection to the recent spate of murders; he assured the bench that these would be resolved once McTavish, the scrap dealer, had been apprehended and further arrests made. In conclusion, he congratulated himself and his colleagues for a job well done.

"Mr Timpkins, do you have anything to add for the defence?"

The young lawyer stuttered, "B-bo-both defendants offer the same defence, my lord. They assure me they had nothing to do with the crime and that it must be a case of mistaken identity." He fell silent.

Lord Haddington looked irritated as he raised his eyes from his book. "Do the accused have anything to say?"

William and Zander spoke in unison. "It wisny me."

Flossie sighed and supressed a tear.

The Sheriff shook his head, before passing sentence.

40. A Debt Repaid
Sunday

Arabella Deveraux

That morning, Arabella's first task was to pack her expensive dresses. She wasn't sad to give up such charming accommodation. Its high vantage point with views across the Firth and river. Mr Black had visited her the day before and explained that everything in the town was as it needed to be and her job was done.

She had borrowed her maid's clothes and had dressed down for today's visit. No makeup, threadbare headscarf and shawl.

On the dock beyond in the early afternoon light, a frigate was being scraped, caulked and refitted in preparation for its next voyage. On the water, a steamer, the deck crowded with sailors and porters stowing, rolling and coiling, clearing the deck of clutter. She would embark on it the following day to return to the continent. A piercing whistle sounded as it prepared to berth. Arabella pulled the shawl over her head and set off.

On turning into Vinegar Close, she almost bumped into Lark leading a group of noisy, scrawny children, heading for the docks and the Floating Chapple. Arabella stood aside to let them pass. Those green eyes, Arabella would recognise them anywhere.

She found the McColligans' door and tapped. Flossie answered, clutching a pile of laundry. Then dropped it, hands shooting to her mouth. She stepped back, rubbed her eyes and looked again.

"No. Su… surely not."

Arabella beamed. "You look as if you have seen a ghost, Flossie."

"Jeanie, oh wee Jeanie. I… It must be… be what? Fifteen years?"

They fell into each other's arms and hugged.

"Hello, sister," said Arabella. "Maybe you should invite me in."

By the fire they held each other. Cried and spluttered, a tangle of words with waves of emotion. Tears of joy at reconciliation, and of sorrow for the years lost. Flossie put the iron cauldron on the hearth and insisted Arabella had the chair with the padding before pulling herself onto a stool at the table.

"So," said Flossie. She took a deep breath. "Where have you been? I assumed you were dead."

"Been a long time, Flossie, so best I start from the beginning. With the man who was both of our first love. The day before they executed Earnest, I visited him."

Flossie's eyes widened. "But you'd gone by then, weeks before, when Father threw you oot and attacked you in the street."

"Days prior to Father's attack, I'd had a fallout with Earnest. He revealed to me how he felt about you, and that our relationship was no more. Such a shock, though I had always known you were the one he really loved. I was so upset, confused, bewildered and angry, I upped sticks and left him without saying a thing."

"But how did Earn—"

"A matter of days after our relationship ended, I discover I'm pregnant. I made a dreadful mistake in telling Father. He fell into a frenzy and came at me with a poker. Thought he would kill me, so I ran. He never offered me the chance to explain. I was lost. I knew Earnest didn't want me and I couldn't return to our family with Dad so furious. I hated everybody, including you. I stole Father's savings to keep me going until I could establish myself elsewhere. I moved away and stayed out of sight with a friend."

"B-but what abou…"

Arabella held up her hands.

"A few weeks later, I learned Earnest was in prison and set to hang. Despite my anger, I considered it only honourable to tell him of my pregnancy. The truth was, I still loved him and believed it may help if he went to his maker with the knowledge that his family line would continue with my child. Decided I owed him that even though he had treated me so badly."

"Oh Jeanie, Jeanie," said Flossie, looking flustered. "How awful, I never kent, I'd no idea. I… I might ne…"

Arabella put her hand on Flossie's arm.

"The evening before the executions, I returned to Leith under cover of darkness. Paid the jailer at the Tollbooth to allow us to meet in his cell. I told him he was the father of my child. He was happy, overjoyed. Said sorry for his treatment of me and that if he had known

I was pregnant, it may have been different. His final act was to pick at the threads on his sleeve, and pull this from the lining of his coat."

Arabella thrust her hand into her skirts and withdrew a small mother-of-pearl box with a red dragon design. Flossie opened it and lifted out the huge sparkling stone, a beautiful blue sapphire.

"The missing jewel," said Flossie, wide-eyed. "The yin the pirates stole and was never found, you had it all the time." Her expression softened.

"Earnest said it was for the bairn," said Arabella. "He even told me where he concealed this little box in which to keep it. Then he said something odd."

Flossie rose, lifted the caldron from the hearth and poured. "Whit did he say that was so strange?" She carried the teapot to the table.

"He said that whatever transpires in the future, he would always watch over the bairn."

Flossie glanced up, a tremble in her voice. "But I dinnae understand. Whit happened to your baby?"

"Four months later, I miscarried, the infant stillborn. I've never been able to have any others."

"But I dinnae follow." Flossie sounded confused. She replaced the jewel and pushed the box back to Arabella.

Arabella returned it to Flossie's hand. "Said it was for his bairn, and we both know who that is."

Flossie hesitated. "How did you…"

"A year back, in Marseilles, I met a Leith sailor who used to live in Vinegar Close. Told me you had a daughter that looked different from your boys. I wondered when he described her, then I saw her, there was no doubt. She's beautiful, looks just like him. Would recognise those green eyes anywhere; that gave it away more than anything."

Flossie smiled. "Aye, she is."

"And you need to give her this," said Arabella, rising.

"I've kept that secret for a long time. I'm amazed my drunken husband never noticed the differences between her and the other four."

"I have to go, Flossie; I'm returning to France tomorrow. I'd never intended to come back to Leith, but my employers needed me here, so I took the opportunity to return and repay the debt. It's what Earnest would have wanted."

Flossie stood, a tear forming in her eye. "Of all the ludicrous things. Earnest, Abraham, our father. Stupid bloody men and the trouble they cause. Cannae you stay? I could use having my sister as a neighbour."

"A different time back then," said Arabella. "A different world. My work here is done—France is my home now—but I'll keep in touch. I can help. Will send you money to find somewhere nicer than Vinegar Close, or your family can come to Marseilles, if you like. I'm finished here. My employer has what he wants, and I am no longer needed."

"Your employer?" said Flossie with a confused glance.

"Don't ask," said Arabella.

Arabella stepped forwards. Flossie put her arms round her sister and smiled. They hugged then kissed for a final time before Arabella slipped out the door.

"Goodbye, Flossie."

"Goodbye, Jeanie."

41. The Gift
Monday

Lark and Charlie Preston

Flossie had sought out anything suitable, the most threadbare clothes among their meagre collection. A pair of William's smelly, aged breeches and a shirt with a torn sleeve. He wouldn't need them again.

"Off you go."

Lark skipped out the door, happier than Flossie could ever remember seeing her.

"Dinnae drown," said Flossie.

Lark beamed as she passed the bottom of Cherry Tree House steps, pulled a pinch of tobacco out of her pocket and handed it to Grannie O'Malley. Grannie nodded, hacked, spat, then watched Lark skip out the courtyard.

"Huh," said Tin Pan Aggie, "would you see the state of her? Miss La De Da looking like an auld scarecrow."

"Aye," said Grannie. "Some folk have nae shame."

***

Tommy and Charlie, river sludge to their knees, stopped and stood still in the weak sunshine, tried to decipher the sound among the quayside noise of thumping engines, groaning cranes, trundling carts of wine and shouting porters. A clunking, the scraping of metal on the cobbles.

"Whit is it? Whit's that clanging?" said Charlie.

Tommy shrugged.

Groups of stevedores and customs men on the jetty were now stopping work to gawk. An officer on horseback at the front, then two uniforms on foot, before the group came into view, a long line of dishevelled, grumbling prisoners making their way along the Shore. Shackled by chain from ankle to waist, hands manacled. A big overseer with a wicked-looking cat-o'-nine-tails swung the whip onto the roadway with a loud crack.

"Keep moving, you horrible lot."

Beyond the signal tower, their ship, the *Asia*, was at the far end of the pier. Soon, the prisoners would be packed into the lower decks like cattle. The convicts hobbled with small steps restricted by the iron on their ankles. An old man stumbled and fell, tried to rise, cried out as a screaming guard lashed him. A ragged woman helped him struggle to his feet.

"Ouch," said Tommy. "Rather him than me."

Charlie beamed.

"Whit's so funny?"

Charlie pointed as Lark appeared, running along the wharf in grubby rags. He waved. Lark slithered down the ladder; the slime oozed through her toes as she stepped between a clinker-built jolly boat and carvel-styled longboat sitting on the mud.

"Yuck. It stinks."

"Whit did he say? Whit were you telt?" shouted Charlie.

"Aye, we can!" cried Lark.

"You can whit?" said Tommy, confused.

"Maw asked the minister," shouted Lark, "and he said it's allowed, so we can. She also says she has a special present from an auld auntie I've never met. Wouldn't tell me whit it is; she wants to give us it both together."

"You can whit?" said Tommy, sounding exasperated.

"You can marry your cousin," said Lark.

Charlie raised his hands in the air and howled like a wolf.

"What of William?" said Tommy.

"We won't have to fret aboot William," said Lark. She turned, pointed at the quay. "See there, six from the end of the line? The ugly mug and shaved head, and Big Zander attached behind. Maw always said that pair were inseparable."

"Where's he going?" asked Charlie.

Lark smiled. "He will be awa for a while. The magistrate condemned him to seven years transportation—to Australia."

Charlie laughed. "Ouch, couldn't have happened to a nicer laddie."

"Nobody's too upset," said Lark. "Maw has washed her hands of him."

"What about Archie?" said Charlie.

"Not been seen by anybody, not a trace. The court put a warrant oot for his capture. Doubt he will get far, reckon it's just a question of time."

The thin cloud above broke; Lark's hair gleamed gold as a ray of sun burst through. She stepped carefully forwards, lifting her legs high with each step. Charlie and Tommy laughed at her ungainly wobble. She halted and glanced down, put her hands in the quagmire and plucked out a scrap of fabric, a miniature leather bag. She tugged the string and a golden guinea dropped into her palm.

"Oooh," said Tommy. "I cannae believe it—Lady Luck on your first time oot."

Charlie moved forward, grabbed her in his arms and offered a slobbery, muddy kiss. Larked laughed and pushed him away.

"Am I embarrassing you?"

"Aye, but dinnae stop."

Charlie took a step back and grinned.

"Look at you," he said. "You…" He thought a moment. "You mudlark."

Historical Notes

(**SPOILER ALERT**: these notes may give away some of the novel's plot lines.)

People

William McColligan

William McColligan of Leith, aged 16, was charged with two counts of theft including that of a handkerchief. He pled guilty along with Alexander McFarlane (also 16) and was sentenced to seven years transportation to Australia. The court found them "with the aggravation of being habit and repute thieves" and had previously been caught stealing shoes and toys.

His record is available online: https://stors.tas.gov.au/CON31-1-7$init=CON31-1-7p355

They both sailed to the other side of the world on the transport ship the *Asia*. William was sent to Point Puer in Tasmania, where trouble seemed to follow him. He fought with other boys and was punished with strokes of the cane as well as hard labour and chain gangs.

He would have been eligible for release in February 1842, but there is no record of whether he returned or stayed.

Dr Thomas Aitchison Latta

Dr Thomas Latta (1796 –1833) was a Leith-based medical pioneer who was responsible for the introduction of the saline solution ("saline drip") method.

To the modern eye, medical practice in the early 1800s looks pretty medieval. While some advances had been made, it was very far from the level of service and expertise we know today. Treatments for a range of ailments included the power of prayer, a "change of air" or purgation by bleeding to clear "impurities" from the body. A limited range of medications were available. The medical profession also suffered from a poor reputation. Many believed them responsible for the problems with body snatchers like Burke and Hare. There are reports of some doctors being attacked by angry mobs.

Cholera was thought to be caused by rancid food, by cold fruits such as cucumbers and melons or by extreme fear or rage. During the cholera pandemic of 1832, Latta learned that people with the illness lost a large portion of their water and salts. He had the skill and bravery to put theory into practice and performed intravenous injections for the first time. Latta saved around a third of his patients. There was a rapid acceptance of this significant medical advancement.

A year after the introduction of his revolutionary treatment, Dr Latta was dead, from consumption, in October 1833. When the pandemic passed, the idea of intravenous fluid replacement then fell out of fashion for the next 50 years, and he received little recognition for his ground-breaking work. A street on the site of the old Eastern General Hospital is now named after him.

Adam White
Adam White was independent Leith's first Lord Provost, elected in 1833. His business interests were initially in herring curing and barrel making before expanding into tar, butter and sheep shearing. Later, he moved into Baltic trading, eventually becoming the director of several local shipping companies and an elder of South Leith Church.

Superintendent Andrew Angus
Andrew Angus was chief of Leith Police from 1832 until 1843, having previously been assistant chief.

Other

Cholera Pandemic
The Asiatic cholera pandemic lasted from 1826 to 1837 and stretched from India to Europe, the Americas, China and Japan, causing more deaths more quickly than any other epidemic disease. The pandemic reached the UK in December 1831, entering through Sunderland. As a port, Leith had actually prepared better than most, though the disease eventually entered Edinburgh through Haddington rather than by sea.

In 1854, John Snow identified a contaminated well in Soho, London, and his research eventually proved cholera was a waterborne disease.

Industrial Revolution
The first Industrial Revolution began in the UK in the late 1700s, starting with mechanised spinning. What followed was a rapid introduction of steam power and factories. Massive urban and population growth followed, combined with very poor working and living conditions for many. References to factory and housing conditions in the novel are all taken from primary UK sources of the time.

The SS *Sirius*, built in Robert Menzies' shipyard in Leith became the first steamship ever to cross the Atlantic in 1837.

Transportation of Convicts
The first convict ships arrived in Australia in 1788, the last in January 1868. Over a period of 80 years, more than 162,000 convicts were transported to Australia, often for the most minor of crimes.

Executions
The last public execution of pirates on Leith Sands was in 1822.

Fraternities, Friendly Societies and Trade Corporations
Many of these groups were formed throughout the UK in the 18th and 19th centuries for the mutual benefit of the members, e.g. the Brotherly Society of Coopers of Leith or the Tranent Benevolent Society of Colliers. In Leith, the ancient societies had a long history, with evidence the ancient trade associations of carters, weavers, tailors and cordiners (shoemakers) were operating in the 1500s and likely much earlier, prior to the Protestant Reformation. The latter two claim to have been founded in 1398.

Kirk Session
A Protestant institution with the task of intervening in the community to ensure services were provided and high moral standards were met. Usually consisted of the parish minister and local elders who were often landowners, merchants or wealthier tradesmen. Kirk Sessions were finally abolished in 1929 with the introduction of town and district councils.

Dwale
An herbal anaesthetic in use since medieval times.

Pollution
In the mid-1800s, a Royal Commission on the sewage of towns reported that:

"The increasing pollution of the rivers and streams of the country is an evil of national importance which urgently demands the application of remedial measures; that the discharge of sewage and the noxious refuse of factories into them is a source of nuisance and danger to health.

Dr. Stevenson Macadam commented on the hideous contamination of the Water of Leith 'Into this small stream is discharged the sewage of the inhabitants of Edinburgh, and the people of Leith, and the result has been that the Water of Leith has become a foul polluted stream, conveying matter of the most disgusting and abominable character, and evolving fetid emanations into the surrounding atmosphere.

That the inhabitants of the districts bordering on the water complained bitterly of the offensive odours from the water, which gave rise to nausea and sickness, and compelled them to keep their doors and windows shut.'

Professor James Simpson commented 'The mortality in the streets bordering on the river, as compared with that away from its banks has a greater death rate in the immediate neighbourhood of the river than at a short distance away. Results are supported by the testimony of many persons who speak of the nausea and sickness brought on by the gases and vapours evolved from the water, and to the general ill health connected.

The condition of the Thames at London is much less foul than the Water of Leith as it traverses Edinburgh. It will thus be observed that the Water of Leith as it leaves Edinburgh contains fully ten times the quantity of organic matter which is found in the Thames at London Bridge, and the offensiveness of the water must be correspondingly greater.'"

The Floating Chapple
Situated in the Old West Dock. From 1820, the chapel offered a place for seamen to worship and also day schooling for the poorest youngsters who "infested the docks", slept rough, dressed in rags and relied on begging and stealing for food.

And...
The Stinking Pig, Fraternity of Unholy Blood and Cherry Tree House are creations of the author's imagination and there is no evidence that

they existed. Though, who knows what's lost in the swirling mists of time? Maybe they did.

The Author

William Haddow, a retired social worker, was born and spent much of his life in Edinburgh (though he is a foreigner to Leith, having been brought up in Meadowbank/Portobello). *Leithers – Two Families* is his second novel.

***

What did you think of Leithers: Two Families?

A big thank you for purchasing this book. It means a lot that you chose this book specifically from such a wide range on offer. I do hope you enjoyed it.

Book reviews are incredibly important for an author. All feedback helps them improve their writing for future projects and for developing this edition. If you are able to spare a few minutes to post a review on Amazon, that would be much appreciated.

Printed in Dunstable, United Kingdom